1ˢᵗ vts
5 —

A Murder Waiting to Happen

Also by L. A. Taylor:

Poetic Justice
Love of Money
Shed Light on Death
Deadly Objectives
Only Half a Hoax
Footnote to Murder

A Murder Waiting to Happen

L. A. Taylor

Walker and Company
New York

First published in the United States of America in 1989 by the Walker Publishing Company, Inc.

Published simultaneously in Canada by Thomas Allen & Son Canada, Limited, Markham, Ontario.
Library of Congress Cataloging-in-Publication Data
Taylor, L. A. (Laurie Aylma) 1939–
    A murder waiting to happen / L. A. Taylor.
       p.   cm.
    ISBN 0-8027-5725-1
    I. Title.
    PS3570.A943M87 1989
    813'.54--dc19   88-26043
                                        CIP

Printed in the United States of America.
10 9 8 7 6 5 4 3 2 1

Minneapolis can provide the traveler many places to stay the night, but the Wellesford Regal is not among them, under its own or any other name. The people who stayed, played, or worked at the Wellesford Regal one fine October weekend are equally fictitious.

So is the snake.

A Murder Waiting to Happen

First

OUTSIDE, CAR DOORS slammed. Dan Bascombe uncrossed his legs, got to his feet, and crossed the room to peer between the narrow slats of the window blind. "It's Wade and Maureen," he reported with a sigh.

"Thank God," someone in the room behind him said. "Maybe now we can get some real work done."

"They can't blame it on traffic this time," added someone else. "It was clear all the way from downtown."

Bascombe, tapping one foot, watched the sleek blond woman stop to admire the generous swath of yellow and red and orange tulips just coming into bloom under the birch tree in his front yard. The man with her touched her waist. Smiling, she turned. As they linked arms and resumed their amble toward the house, Bascombe strode to the front door and yanked it open only to find that the couple hadn't yet mounted the steps.

"Move it, can't you?" he called. "You're already half an hour late."

"Keep your shirt on," the man said mildly.

Maureen Tesla glanced coolly at Bascombe as she entered, and stepped past him into the living room with the confident smile of a woman sure of her looks. She measured out an equal portion of that smile for each of the eleven people staring impatiently at her as she wriggled her shoulders to shed her jacket, which Bascombe snatched as it fell.

"Oh," she said, arching her delicate brows. "Are we the last?"

"As usual," muttered one of the other women, glancing

fiercely at the notebook in her lap.

Bascombe leaned the closet door shut on the coats. "Let's get on with it," he said. "Coffee?" At the newcomers' nods, he yelled, "Helen? Two more coffees," and crossed the small room to sit cross-legged with his back against the glass fireplace screen. Several piles of papers had been arranged on the hearth near his knees. While Maureen and Wade settled into virtually the same spot on the floor, Bascombe pulled a sheet off the top of each pile and shook them into a single stack.

"We've got about ten zillion things to take care of before this convention comes off," he said, handing the stack to Wade Yates. "If you two can't get here on time, we'll just have to go ahead and make decisions without you. Con's coming up in five months."

"Christ, half an hour!" Yates complained, settling back in front of the window as Bascombe made up a second packet of papers. "Can't you hang on that long? We want some input here, too. Can we help it if the traffic was heavy?"

"Yates, you volunteered for the organizing committee," one of the other men told him, while two of the women exchanged glances. "Nobody asked you. So you could get here on time like the rest of us, instead of holding everybody up."

"Or *you* could quit," Yates suggested.

"Cool it," Bascombe advised. "Let's get going—Oh, thanks, Helen." Bascombe's wife set down two fresh mugs of coffee, refilled two or three others as they were held out to her, and withdrew with a nod and a smile.

"Sue gave us the hotel committee's report before you got here," Bascombe continued, clearly well in charge although he was the smallest of the men present. "We've got the core and the north wing. They gave us a good price and agreed to our needs. As soon as our lawyer looks it over, we'll sign the contract."

2

"The core and the north wing?" Yates asked. "What about the east wing? I thought we wanted the view."

Sue Evers, the woman taking notes, looked up. "It was the north wing or find another hotel, and we can't afford anything super ritzy. If we want to keep it cheap, the Wellesford Regal is it, and they've already got another group booked that weekend," she explained. "Engineers, I think."

"Ooo, mundanes!" Maureen lifted her head from her companion's shoulder and grinned eagerly. "Fun, fun, fun!"

Bascombe stared at her a moment. She dropped her eyes and shrugged. Her wavy golden yellow hair glinted as it shifted on her shoulders, giving the gesture a calculated look.

"This is the first year for Twin-Con," Bascombe said, very calm. "We don't want to get a rep for hassling mundanes like some other cons have. Makes it hard to come back to the same hotel. I don't know about you, but I want to go back. It makes the planning simpler, and the place is cheap."

"But the mundanes are half the fun," Maureen protested. "And what's the harm?"

"Some mundanes can't take a joke." Bascombe spoke with the soft patience usually reserved for dealing with a child. "They get uptight when they're minding their own business and Darth Vader draws a laser on them." His dark eyes were still locked on Maureen, who settled back, pouting. "Then they give the hotel management hell. The very same hotel management we want to do business with. So at the very least the concom members can leave them alone, even if we can't get the fans to do it." Maureen shrugged again. "I mean it, Maureen."

"The hotel's hiring a couple of rent-a-cops to keep everybody happy," Sue interrupted. "They pay, so we don't care."

3

"Fascists," said the man who had spoken earlier.

"Which," Bascombe said loudly over the resulting protests and agreements, "brings us to our first decision of the night. Weapons policy. The promos are going to the printer before our next meeting so we have to decide now. I propose we adopt the policy Minicon uses—class one and two lasers only, no real-looking guns, no projectiles. Edged blades safety-sheathed—"

"Wait a minute."

The same man again. Bascombe bit back a sigh. "Yes, Cass?"

"Why do we have to do *anything* the way Minicon does?"

"Because we have yet to hold one convention, and they've been at it for over twenty years, and what they do works."

"Sucks."

"Works," Bascombe repeated, unaroused.

Cass Grenzman was one of the invaders, as Bascombe thought of them. The original idea had simply been to have a second large convention for Minnesota science fiction fans. Minicon was huge and satisfying but came only once a year, in the spring. The new con would be held in the fall, providing a supplement to the much smaller meetings scattered through the rest of the year.

The heart of Bascombe's organization, those who bore most of the financial load, had begun with only that one idea in mind. As word spread, a few more people asked to help. Some of them brought experience in organizing and were welcome. Then the others had come—his "invaders": people who had fits over Minicon's tried-and-true policies and joined the new organization hoping for something different. They came in two varieties: those who wanted a more protected environment and those, like Cass, who wanted absolute freedom. Bascombe stifled a yawn. Wade

Yates and Cassius Grenzman between them could turn sixty seconds into an hour any day of the week. Bascombe had been within a hair of resigning as convention committee chairman when he'd learned that both had volunteered to serve on it. Unfortunately, by that time he had already taken out the loan.

Topping Grenzman and Yates, if that were even possible, was Desmond Donovan. Already this evening, Helen had run out to the nearby PDQ to buy decaf coffee at Diz's request, and the jerk *still* hadn't been happy because the coffee was the wrong brand of instant and probably tainted with some kind of solvent. Bascombe glanced at Donovan—whose hot water and milk cooled untouched on the table beside him—and then at his watch. Seven-thirty-five. A young eternity had passed since seven.

"Minicon gets fifteen hundred people," Grenzman said. "We won't have that many, will we?"

"I hope to hell not," Bascombe said. "We wouldn't begin to know where to put them. But right now, *please*— the topic is weapons policy."

As anyone who'd seen this crew in action for the last couple of months might have predicted, that started them off again.

"Okay," the chairman broke in after ten minutes of exceedingly vigorous discussion. "We'll vote on each regulation separately."

This stroke of genius reduced the time it took to come to agreement to a mere half hour. Lasers would be restricted; real-looking guns were not, except that no real guns, loaded or unloaded, would be allowed. That regulation was amended to include all projectile weapons, in particular crossbows, and further amended to permit projectile weapons other than guns only if either they were disabled or no ammunition was brought. A proposal to permit flintlocks was defeated. Edged blades, on the other hand, sheathed but unsecured, would be permitted.

Bascombe, no favorer of weapons of any sort, felt he had won as much of a victory as he could expect. After all, the main reason some of these people were crowded into his living room on an otherwise gorgeous late spring night was dissatisfaction with the weapons restrictions of Minicon, although he imagined he knew what the insurance company and the attorney would think of the new policies.

Run it past the pros before the promos went to the printer. Come back to the next concom meeting with the changes made. Tell the committee *ex post facto* that without a stricter policy there would be no con.

"Now," he said, willing himself not to flinch. "We come to the question of security. Diz?"

Diz Donovan let his raised hand float downward. "Food worries me," he half-whispered, his balding forehead rucked up under wisps of faded brown hair. "All these people reaching into the same popcorn buckets. God knows what kind of diseases they might spread. We should make them wear plastic gloves."

"Gloves!" one of the women exclaimed. "Next you'll have us wearing surgical masks."

"Good idea," Donovan agreed.

"I think we can leave food problems to the refreshments committee," Bascombe said.

"You people haven't taken a single one of my suggestions in the last three months," Donovan complained, glowering.

"You got a single one that makes sense?" Cass Grenzman demanded. "Let's hear it."

Donovan's fists tensed. "That's an interesting point you've made there, Diz," Bascombe said hurriedly. "But I think you ought to take it to the refreshments committee. It's really their business."

Donovan's fists loosened and his usual vague expression

reclaimed his face. "Now, about security . . . "

"The hotel's hiring rent-a-cops, Sue says. That should be plenty," Grenzman declared.

"The cops are a problem all by themselves." Yates tugged at his long mustache as he spoke, a habit that drove Bascombe silently up the wall. He looked away, only to find Donovan smoothing *his* mustache. Bascombe's upper lip started to itch. He clenched his fingers.

"They're not fans," Yates continued. "Ten to one they've never seen an sf con before. They find some of our weirdos floating around talking to people they can't see, they'll get a little uptight, you know?" Fortunately, Diz Donovan missed Yates's sideways glance. "I think we need a good security arrangement of our own."

"We should outlaw Killer," Donovan blurted. Now everybody looked at him.

"Yes, Killer does present a problem," Bascombe allowed.

"Never do it." Grenzman shook his head. "Even if you say no, which if I'm on this committee you won't, people're gonna play Killer anyway."

"You should know, macho macho," Yates said.

"Listen, man, it's a great game."

"Bunch of druggies chasing each other around like little kids. Sick, if you ask me."

"Nobody did."

"Plain sick."

"Try it, soldier boy. You might like it."

"I don't need to try any of your—"

"Okay, okay." Bascombe made shushing motions while Donovan sat openmouthed, staring at Grenzman. "We'll get back to that later. Right now I'm talking about checking badges to keep the engineers out of our beer, things like that. Maybe an overnight cop for the hucksters. Let's keep on track. Time's getting away from us."

"We wouldn't need any security if we outlawed Killer," Donovan insisted.

"Later, Diz, okay?"

"If we outlaw Killer," Donovan nearly shouted, "we won't get any of that scum that comes just to play it."

"Watch your mouth, dry balls."

"I don't need to play sick games to make me feel—"

"Diz, shut up. Cass, sit down. Christ, is this the famous friendly fandom of science fiction?"

"Friendly fans don't need security," said a kid in the corner who hadn't breathed a word for the last three meetings.

"Checking badges is just to keep the non-fans out," Sue said. "And the teenagers from getting plastered."

"All we need is volunteers for that. And we don't need a cop in the huckster room." Grenzman.

"Like it or not, sometimes even a fan gets tempted," Bascombe pointed out. "There's some expensive stuff in that room. Not just the artwork. With any luck, we'll get a couple of jewelers, and there's that guy with the swords—"

"Yeah," said Grenzman.

"And," Bascombe continued, raising his voice, "some of those collectors would practically kill for an early *Astounding* or a first-edition Tolkien. We won't get the hucksters coming if we can't guarantee they won't get ripped off, and if they don't show, there goes our space rent and consignment money. Do I have to remind you that some of us could go broke on this project?"

A little shiver went around the room, shared by those who had put up their own cash as seed money for the con and hoped at least to clear enough to pay themselves back. Grenzman, Bascombe remembered, was not one of them, as anyone could tell when he opened his mouth—again.

The argument—bitter, as any fundamentally philosophical argument can be—continued for almost an hour. Bas-

8

combe kept out of it. He gazed instead at the walls he had papered with the faint blue stripe his wife had chosen only a month before, walls of an admittedly tiny house in which he nevertheless took pride. He considered it evidence of his commitment to the cause that he had put this house up as collateral for the loan he'd used as his share of the seed money. He could, instead, have sold some of the books lined up on shelf after shelf in his dry, warm, not very big cellar. Some of those the collectors would practically kill for, but nobody sells old friends.

In the end, the concom agreed to hire an outsider to supervise security, and three people—two pro- and one anti-security—were appointed to interview candidates.

"Tell you what," Bascombe suggested, taking charge again. "Let's look in this year's Yellow Pages and last year's Yellow Pages and find somebody new in the business."

"What for?"

"He'll be hungry, maybe, and maybe give us a good deal."

Murmurs of assent went around the circle. Out in the dining room, the clock on the sideboard struck once. Nine-thirty. "Okay, that's done," Bascombe said. "Now—"

"Just a minute."

"Cass?"

"I want to go on record that I opposed this whole thing."

"It shall be so recorded," Sue Evers said dryly, writing with a flourish, and Bascombe went on, with relief, to other business.

The clock on the sideboard again struck once, this time for twelve-thirty. "Two swallows won't hurt the baby," Helen Bascombe remarked to her husband. She reached for the bottle of beer on the table between them and poured an inch into her glass, where only a few drops of mineral water remained.

He grinned at her, not quite daring to believe in the baby. They had waited so long, and she was still so slender.

"Sounded kind of loud down here sometimes," she said.

"Right." Dan sighed. "I just hope I can get everyone moving in the same direction in time to keep this con from turning into a fiasco. Some of them seem to think it will all smooth out by magic. There's really only five us of paying enough attention to what we're doing—the ones that put up the money."

"Well, I can save you some trouble," Helen said. "While you guys were fighting about the T-shirts I looked at the Yellow Pages. There's only one new security agency since last year, and they're downtown, right near the hotel. Not only that, they don't say anything about ever being with the FBI, which ought to save a few fireworks."

"Who's that?"

She yawned. "Some outfit called Forrester Associates."

Chapter One

I MADE A tight U-turn and followed the sporty lime green hood over my snarling motor south to see a dusty blue, highly antique Honda Civic drift to the curb in front of my house. Mack Forrester shouldered open the reluctant driver's-side door. Mildly surprised, I killed the lawn mower engine, left the machine sitting in the middle of the grass, and strolled over.

"Hi, J.J. Collided with any automated Frisbees lately?" he asked, urging the car door shut with his butt.

"Not that I noticed."

UFOs, Mack meant. In real life, I'm a computer software engineer, but when the spirit and the little green men move me, I'm the local field investigator for an outfit called the Committee for Analysis of Tropospheric and Celestial Happenings—CATCH, for short—which is a fancy way of saying I check out UFO sightings. After eleven years of looking, I'll admit that I've found one or two things I can't explain—yet. I've also found a lot of people who don't know the planet Venus from a hole in the sky, seventeen weather balloons, more airplanes than I can count, a stupendous sighting of gulls over Lake Harriet three blocks from my house in southwest Minneapolis, and at least a dozen hoaxes. I've been led into altogether too many close encounters of the off-the-wall kind and not one for-sure flying saucer in the lot. Mack, lifelong buddy that he is, can't leave it alone.

Now he squinted into the endless blue of an early fall afternoon and turned in a slow circle. Circle complete, he sadly shook his head. "Me, neither," he said. "Ah, well, maybe tomorrow."

I am forgiving. Even magnanimous. "Want a beer?"

"Sure, but it can wait till you get that last patch of lawn mowed."

I hauled on the starting cord a couple of times, got a blast of noise and blue smoke from the mower, and made four passes across my yard while Mack sat on the front steps watching.

"Now you can come do mine," he said, when the engine died.

"You got a kid ought to be big enough by now," I pointed out.

"He is, but he wants money."

Mack got up and trailed me to the garage while I put the mower away. I see more of him now that he quit the police force and started his own detective agency. He'd had plans for law school that got quietly dropped. Instead, he was taking computer science courses at the University a couple of nights a week. Meanwhile, Forrester Associates—Mack and his answering machine—attempted to buy the groceries for a family of five. How that worked out I don't know and don't ask, especially since Mack's wife went to work at the Edina Laundry, feeding wet sheets into a gigantic ironer she calls "the six roll" from early morning to midafternoon.

"I hear you're addressing a convention next month," Mack said, holding my back screen door open for me. "Hot stuff."

"Where'd you hear that?"

"Where do you think?"

I headed straight for the refrigerator. "You got one of their flyers? When did you start reading science fiction, let alone get on a fan mailing list?"

"I'm not."

12

"How'd you find out, then?"

"I got ways," Mack said. He rocked on his heels, arms folded, eyes narrowed. TV cop stuff.

"What, you got your answering machine secondhand from the FBI?" I slipped the neck of a bottle of Blatz under the old Coke bottle opener Karen found in a junk shop and screwed to our kitchen wall, and levered the cap off.

"Something like that," Mack said, taking the beer. "As a matter of fact, I got you the job."

"Come again?"

The "job" was an invitation to address a science fiction convention on the subject of UFO reports. The invitation had surprised me some. I'm not much of a science fiction reader, and I'd never heard of this convention, but it was right in town and looked like an easy fifty bucks so I said yes. Then they asked me if I'd take part in a panel discussion the next morning. I'd said yes to that, too, and they'd thrown in free tickets to the con, as they call it, for me and my wife.

"Seriously," Mack said. "They hired me to do security for this blast. While we were hashing out the details, I mentioned you and your saucers, and the guy said, yeah, he'd read about you in the newspaper, the con didn't have any reputation yet and they were short a couple of speakers, maybe they'd invite you to give a talk. Saw your name in the program that came in the mail yesterday."

"Thanks," I said.

"J.J., do us both a favor? This is my first decent-size job. It's gonna make or break my whole reputation. So *please* don't find any bodies?" Mack took his first mouthful of cold Blatz. "Ah, that's good."

"I don't plan to find bodies, Mack." I had my own beer now, and I washed down the nasty taste of the sentence with a quick swallow.

"They just fall out of the closet at you. Yeah, I know."

"I never found one in a closet." A guy in his living room, yes, but never a closet. "Besides, what could go wrong at a science fiction convention? The fans I've met, guys at work, seem like a pretty mild bunch compared to the kind you encounter so-called studying UFOs. The guy that talked to me seemed to be in full possession of his senses."

"Bring the beer," Mack said, motioning with his head toward the family room beyond the kitchen. He chose the recliner, which groaned when he sat down. Mack's a big, square, fair, hairy guy who can make an average Joe like me feel like a midget. He leaned his forearms on his knees, turning the bottle in his hands.

"What's up?"

"I'm having second thoughts." Mack sat with his lower lip bulged out under a tight mouth for a few seconds. "It doesn't look like the piece of cake I thought it was."

"What's the problem?"

"Problems. Problems, multiple. First of all, like any other convention, half of them plan to get drunk out of their skulls. That I figured on. But come to find out these guys carry weapons. Just decoration, the concom—listen to me, I'm talking like one of them—convention committee chairman tells me. Christ, J.J., do you know what a claymore is?"

"Sorry, no."

"Your Scottish forebears may now commence spinning in their graves. It's a Celtic sword. Not one of these chintzy little French jobs they chase each other up and down the steps with on the late late movie. A big, heavy, two-hand, two-edged thing you could take a man's head off with. One swipe."

I felt something cold on the right side of my neck and discovered I'd put my hands up, Blatz and all, to protect it.

"Right," Mack said. "These jokers carry every kind of blade you can imagine, from that on down. Only rule they make, no concealed weapons."

14

"Maybe at the last minute my aged Aunt Fanny can develop a fulminating illness," I mused.

"Wimp." Mack stretched. The lip tightened again. "They tell me nobody gets hurt. I got them to agree to having any kind of knife tied into a scabbard, otherwise security is going to confiscate it until the end of the convention. Holy shit, what a ruckus! I couldn't believe it. You'd think I tried to take the shotguns away from the entire NRA."

"Well, if they're tied in, at least nobody can just yank a blade on the spur of the moment," I said.

Mack looked up, no change in his sober expression. "That's the general idea. But that's not all. They've got guns. Not the real thing, but you should see some of them. Jeez, to look at the plastic .357 magnum one of these guys showed me, I couldn't tell it from my own. Not from two or three yards away. If that. It's weighted, so it carries like the real thing, couple of pounds on the end of your arm. Muzzle flash when it's fired."

"Fired!"

"Fancy cap pistol is all it is." Mack took a swallow of beer. "I wouldn't want to be looking at it over a cash drawer, though, I'll tell you. *Or* at the Uzi submachine gun this same guy showed me, fake or not."

I looked out the back window at the bright bed of zinnias along the back property line. "What do they want those for—besides holdups?"

Mack shrugged. "I can tell you what this guy Grenzman and his buddies do. They play this game they call 'Killer.' I don't quite get it, but the general idea is a bunch of guys stalk each other through the hotel in the middle of the night, and try to knock each other off. I hear some of the games get real fancy. The guys wear light-sensitive vests so when somebody gets shot with a light gun it lights up a bulb on top of his head, and everybody can tell he's dead, check?"

15

"That doesn't sound so bad," I said. "Could be fun."

"For you, maybe," Mack said dubiously. "Not for me. I lived twelve out of the past thirteen years looking to avoid the real thing, and that'll last me all my life. They can keep it."

"I can see that," I agreed.

I got up and went into the kitchen to rummage for some potato chips, without luck; Karen tries to keep us skinny. I glanced at my watch. She'd be back from the supermarket any minute, but she probably wouldn't have any munchies in the bag, unless our son Joey had worn her down.

"Another beer?" I called to Mack.

"Nah, I'm still working on this one."

That's another change in Mack since he quit being a cop. He drinks maybe half as much beer as he used to. Almost puts him in my league.

"What I came over for, J.J.," he said, as I sat down again. "I want you to keep your eyes open at this thing. Tell me if you see anything funny going down. You staying over either night?"

"I wasn't planning to."

"See if you can work something out. 'Specially for Saturday. Sunday morning, midnight to dawn, that's what gives me nightmares. It wouldn't be so bad, only there's another convention there at the same time, and who knows what those guys will be packing? Ten will get you twenty it ain't cap pistols, and when these kids start playing cops and robbers who the hell knows what'll break loose. Plus the hotel is hiring its own security guards, and I know zip about them."

"You want me in the middle of this game? Thanks, Mack, I just changed my mind. Sounds like a real drag."

"You don't have to play the game." Mack gestured with his now-empty bottle. "J.J., I got the worst feeling about this whole thing. I've got to have somebody around I trust. Somebody who notices the little things. They aren't giving me enough money to hire an off-duty cop, so I can't get a pro. All I've got to work with is a bunch of volunteers." Mack shook his head. "College kids, mostly, and a few middle-aged ladies, some of them male. They'll go around, check badges to make sure nobody's crashing their party. Make sure the blades are tied down. Cool down any arguments. If they run into real trouble, I got three, maybe four more volunteers with a little real experience they can call on, and there's me. I'm sleeping over."

"I hope you got a free bed," I said.

"What I got is a fold-up cot in what they call the huckster room. People come to these deals, rent space to sell artwork and books and buttons with mouth-off sayings and what have you. Shit, J.J., there's even a guy sells claymores, just in case you left yours in your other pants."

My turn to frown. That sounded like a Mack-when-he's-worried line. "Lots of stuff worth stealing then," I said.

"Oh, sure. That part's no big deal."

I heard the station wagon pull into the driveway and a door slam. Karen was back from shopping.

"What is, then?"

"I dunno, J.J. Like I say, I've got a feeling. Every time I get together with these guys, there's something I don't like there, and I can't put my finger on it. I blocked as many holes as I can think of, what I could get past that damnfool committee, but I just know there's something I'm missing. And it's not just because I'm a mundane."

"A mundane? What's that?"

Mack grinned briefly. "You and me, pal. Members of the mundane world. Anybody that hasn't bought a ticket to the convention, in other words."

Karen came into the kitchen, sang out a hello to me and to Mack, and went back out, letting the screen door bang.

"I'll keep my eyes open," I said. "But it would help if I knew what I was looking for."

"I don't know, J.J. That's just it. I don't know."

"Well," I said, standing up as Joey ran into the family room and hurled himself at Mack. "Stay cool."

"Check." Mack tousled Joey's hair and levered himself out of the chair with my six-year-old son still clinging to his arm. As he went into the kitchen and said something to Karen I hung back, bothered by something I couldn't put my finger on.

Then I got it. "Stay cool" is usually Mack's advice to me.

Chapter Two

BY THE TIME the convention came around, I regretted I'd agreed to give my talk on UFOs. The weekend promised to be sunny and crisp, as only October can be. A brisk breeze was blowing as I drove home that Friday afternoon, sending all the leaves dashing ahead of my car; a blaze of chrysanthemums billowed over the old stone wall on the corner of my block. Only a fool would stay indoors in weather like this, I told myself. Could be the last picnic weekend of the year. As I turned into my driveway I was wishing we could pack a basket lunch to take to Beard's Pleasance the next day. What could be better than spending the afternoon with Karen and Joey at the playground in that little park or messing around on the shore of Lake Harriet just down the hill?

But my talk, I reminded myself with much annoyance, was scheduled for one o'clock the next afternoon. One day shot. Then the panel Sunday morning. Half of another day shot. Not only that, Mack had been thinking up ridiculous reasons for me to attend the Friday night T-Con festivities at the rate of one every other day, though I'd planned to skip them.

The phone was ringing as I walked in the back door. Mack.

A conference of electrical engineers was meeting at the same hotel that weekend, with an emphasis on new ways of structuring computers. It occurred to me as Mack talked that although I don't have much expertise in computer hardware myself, I'd worked with a number of people who did—people I hadn't seen for a while who might turn up at the conference. That did the trick: at the last minute I gave in. Karen decided to come with me, and after dinner we drove into town. Joey was delighted, as usual, to have the old lady next door come over to babysit.

We'd left the station wagon in the garage under the hotel but somehow had come out on the street, so we used the main entrance. The lobby of the Wellesford had been redecorated when it married glitz and took the surname Regal, not long after the last time I'd been there. The old shabby splendor was gone in favor of more up-to-date glitter: bronze-tinted mirrors with and without gold marbling and enough gold carpet to account for a year's production from some lucky mill. They'd moved the registration desk to where even the uninitiated could find it, and opened up the ground-floor lobby with tall, narrow windows between the Greek-style columns that used to disguise whatever holds the building up. The columns themselves had been disguised in turn, with more mirrors. The doorman ignored us in favor of a tip sheet barely concealed on his desk.

"Well!" Karen said, as she took in the half-block-long chandelier that hid the old cracked ceiling. "Maybe I should have rented a diamond tiara!" Half a second later a pudgy woman wearing nothing but fake bearskin shorts and a fake bearskin poncho thrown precariously over the top ambled past. "I take that back," Karen said. "I'm over-dressed."

Her dark cord skirt and the blue sweater I'd given her the Christmas before looked fine to me, and I said so.

A few steps inside the revolving door, one sign pointed sf fans toward the escalator that had replaced the old marble staircase, and another directed the engineers to the east wing elevators. I followed instructions for the former despite having more sympathy with the latter. I knew what the engineers were in for, at least: a slab of roast beef in a puddle of congealing juice and two hours of a droning speech about something that had sounded fascinating in the advance program.

The fans? I'd soon find out. The chatter of voices in the second-floor reception area carried loudly to the bottom of the escalator.

The staircase the escalator had replaced used to lead into a wide corridor, and a flock of drab, windowless meeting rooms used to open off that. But there'd been remodeling here, too: now we found a fairly large central meeting area (more gold carpet, sturdier than downstairs, but no mirrors). To the right, several doors led into the smaller meeting rooms I remembered; the wall between the corridor and what had once been a cavernous room to the left had simply been moved over twenty feet or so and pierced with more doors, probably so the big room could be divided up when necessary. Ahead, then, would be the narrower corridor that led both to sleeping rooms and to other conference facilities—but that I had to take on faith. My line of sight was, well, blocked.

Dan Bascombe, the chairman of the organizing committee for the affair, had told me to get a badge from the T-Con registration desk and then come find him in the convention offices. Easier said than done. In the large, open area at least a couple of hundred people wandered back and forth. Closer inspection revealed a long line of chatting fans snaking away from the registration table, where two harried-looking young women were checking lists and issuing prepared conventioneers' badges. A slightly shorter line attended a second table set up for people who hadn't preregistered. They apparently got to write out their own badges. Between these lines was a third table, at which Mack and some other guy—a chunky, sandy-haired specimen with a long mustache that framed a quick grin—were sitting. The crowd was too dense for me

21

to see exactly what they were doing.

"I wish I'd brought my notebook," Karen breathed.

I could see why. Karen's a writer, or tries to be. She uses her notebook to write down ideas and odd incidents, with the general notion that one or the other or both will show up in her stories. Certainly plenty of material was walking around here, even if all she wanted to do was describe the people standing in line.

"Lots of characters from TV and the movies," Karen observed.

She was right, though there was even more of a mix than that. Some of the costumes represented characters I knew. I saw Darth Vader replicated four or five times. Some I didn't know: two men in chain mail and a whole clutch of belly dancers, most with plenty of belly. Others required thought, like the pointy-eared people I recognized, after digging around in my early adolescent memories, as Vulcans from *Star Trek*. A bunch of the semi-fur-clad—or should I say fur-semi-clad?—women, some with figures well worth noticing, though I tried not to let Karen catch me at it, wandered through the crowd. One boy in a gleaming costume puzzled me. I couldn't decide if he was meant to be a fifteenth-century knight or somebody in a space suit. He turned to talk to the girl in line behind him, revealing a chunky clear plastic gun with a wavering blue light at the end. Spaceman.

Not that everyone was in costume. Far from it. Most were ordinary-looking people, casually dressed; they looked as bored as anyone does while waiting in line. Others looked happier—they'd found friends to talk to or a place to sit on one of the gleaming mahogany benches that alternated with brass-potted plants near the sides of the room. Beyond the benches, people read the notices posted outside the doors of the meeting rooms or searched through literature stacked on long tables set up against the walls. A surprising number of young and not-so-young children, some sporting bright green badges, darted through the remaining open space, playing tag. I heard a mother yell at her kid not to crawl between people's feet and an answering, "Awww, Mom!"

I did some of my famous observation of minutiae and hoped that the names I saw on the nearby badges were not the ones the wearers had registered with the Social Security Administration. On the other hand, the names on the badges apparently didn't matter. People greeted each other by what sounded like their real names regardless of how they were labeled. On the whole, the crowd tended toward the young side, although I saw some gray heads here and there. The average waistline was probably broader than you'd see in a suburban shopping mall, though I wasn't sure about that.

"There's Mack," Karen said, pitching her voice over the buzz of conversation.

"I know. I saw him."

"I hope this really is a break for him—Joy looks *so* tired lately. Oh, and there's—I forget his name—John something?"

"Ferraro," I said, spotting the man she was pointing at as he spotted me. "Hey, Jack!"

"J.J.!"

Ferraro came over with a big grin and both hands out in greeting. He'd gone through the line and acquired a dayglo pink rectangle to pin where he pleased. I'd seen another applied to the backside of a pair of jeans, but Ferraro's tag was on his T-shirt, a slogan-free, bright red expanse whose color made the pink tag seem to vibrate.

"What do you think of all this?" he asked, waving to include the two lines and the knots of people talking.

"Interesting."

"I meant the turnout. The concom must have done a good job of advertising—this is their first year."

23

"They've drawn a crowd, all right," Karen said.

"Are you here just to give your talk, J.J., or are you a fan?" Ferraro asked.

"Just giving my talk."

"It's not till tomorrow, is it?"

"No. They gave me two free passes, though, and Karen was curious, so we came early." My wife punched me in the back with a stiffened finger for this bald lie, but Ferraro didn't notice.

"I'd have thought you'd be in the other wing," he said. "You're a computer engineer, aren't you?"

"Software," I said. "Those guys over there build the machines—I just talk to them."

"I see," Ferraro said, though he clearly didn't. "You write, don't you?" he said to Karen. "You'll be glad you came. Look for the panel discussions they have about writing. They should be interesting."

"You've gone to other, uh, meetings like this?" Karen asked.

"Oh, I've been going to cons for years." Ferraro's face took on a happy gleam. "There's a great one here in the spring, three or four times the size of this. Then I go to one in Milwaukee some years." The gleam was replaced by lifted brows. "Do either of you read SF?"

"I've read some Asimov," I admitted. "And, uh, Robert Heinlein."

"*I, Robot* and *Stranger in a Strange Land*, and that's it, right?" Ferraro deduced, genially and correctly. "There's more to science fiction than that, believe me."

"I don't doubt it. How's the UFO business?" Ferraro is the chief moving force behind a local amateur UFO study group, one of the few sensible ones around.

"Slow," he said, scanning the crowd. "You know, J.J., I hate to say this, but I'm losing interest. I've been studying UFOs since Ken Arnold reported the things back in nineteen forty-seven. Damn near forty years, since I was eleven years old, and the damn things just slip away and slip away. And now that sightings have dropped off so badly . . . " He shook his head. "I gave up the study group, did you hear?"

"No, I didn't."

"We had our last meeting last spring, the day after J. Allen Hynek died, not that we planned it that way." Ferraro stuck his hands in his pockets and looked at the people around him. "One thing you'll find about this bunch, J.J., ninety-nine percent of them know when they're looking at fantasy. Oh, there's a couple that talk to people you and I can't see, but the rest just happen to like being fans, and most of the time SF doesn't get all tangled up with the real world. These people can still think, you see what I mean?"

The line shifted ahead. Ferraro spotted somebody else he wanted to greet and excused himself. As we got closer to the registration table, I saw that Mack and the other man were asking questions as each person picked up his tag and a packet of papers. One fan nodded. Mack said something.

The guy shook his head.

Mack said something.

The guy pulled a gun on him.

I heard Karen gasp. With no change in his pleasant expression, Mack put his hand out, palm up, and the gun got handed over. Mack wound a wide strip of dayglo green tape around the barrel just back of the muzzle, and the other guy behind the table handed the gun's owner a screaming purple Ping-Pong ball. Mack snipped the tape loose from the roll, stuck the end down, and handed the gun back with a grin. The owner turned away, scowling.

"The gun's not real," I assured Karen. "Mack told me about them. They're plastic cap guns. They just look real." I could see her filing that away in her head in lieu of a notebook.

Our turn came. We got tagged and information-packeted, and the guy with Mack tugged on his Fu Manchu mustache and asked if we had any real-looking weapons.

"No, but I have a neighbor with a dilly of a Luger," I said, looking at Mack.

He pounded his forehead once with a clenched fist. "I do not want to hear anything whatsoever about that woman," he said. "Whatever she is doing now, you can keep it to yourself."

"She's babysitting Joey," I said. Karen was telling the man with the mustache that neither of us had any guns and Mack was an old friend.

"Then I hope to God she's not taking target practice at your back door," Mack said to me, unfairly. It had only been one shot, from inside, and all Mrs. Eskew had done was put a hole in the screen—years ago.

"I doubt it," I said. "What's with the purple Ping-Pong balls?"

"They go on the underside of the barrel whenever the gun's out of the holster," Mack explained. "Marks it a fake from dead on, when you can't see the green tape. See you later."

"Sure."

Karen trailed me as I moved out of the way to get a look at the literature I'd been handed and try to locate Dan Bascombe, the man I'd learned to call the concom chair, to find out what was expected of me the next day. I couldn't find directions to the convention offices anywhere. Karen, peering over my shoulder, finally figured out that the place to go was Suite 231. They'd either know where Bascombe was or would take a message for him.

I caught up with Dan Bascombe, a smallish guy with a smooth black mustache and curly black hair, after the opening ceremonies. He was probably the only man in this wing of the hotel with a white shirt on his back: short sleeves, no tie.

"Hi, welcome," he said, all good cheer. "And this is your wife? Mine's around somewhere. Helen?"

A small, dark-haired woman turned and came toward us, also smiling. "My wife," Bascombe said and introduced us.

Helen Bascombe had the placid glow and thick middle of advancing pregnancy. Karen congratulated her.

Bascombe grinned. "A Christmas baby," he said.

"Helen!" somebody called.

"Go on," said her husband. "See you later. Come on up to the con suite with me, you two," he added. "Have a beer."

We progressed slowly across the large, central room, where people were still registering—and still having their weapons checked by Mack and his aide—while Bascombe greeted his friends. He seemed to know everyone. The walk to the elevator bank became something of a triumphal procession, Bascombe smiling and waving and people reaching out hands.

"I can't believe it's really happening," he said as we got into the elevator with a pair of pretty, dark-haired, pointy-eared twins in floppy red robes. "There were times I thought it was all just a dream and I'd wake up any second."

"Dreams do come true, sometimes," Karen remarked.

"Half the time this one has been a nightmare," Bascombe sighed. "But so far, so good. Punch ten for us, would you, Michelle?"

One of the twins pressed the floor button. The name on her badge was not Michelle. It looked like T'Pong. I examined the other twin's badge. Yup. T'Ping.

"This is where we sometimes have troubles," Dan Bascombe said, as we got off the elevator and followed a series

27

of arrows down several turns of hallway. "The guy doing security for us is a friend of yours, isn't he?"

"Mack Forrester, yes," I said.

"He's mostly here to satisfy the insurance people. They get a little antsy about all that stuff in the huckster room. Fans are friendly types. All we really need is somebody to check badges and make sure they're ours. With only half of the hotel ours, crashers can be a problem. Besides, I'll have to admit, we have our share of drunks."

We sailed past a bored-looking guy perched on a high stool at the door of a suite and straight into bedlam.

"Friday night," Bascombe said over his shoulder. "When you find out who's here."

"Dan, where's the junk food? I'm dying for a Twinkie!" The girl grabbing Bascombe's arm was one of the belly dancers I'd seen downstairs, and was partially clad in bejeweled satin exactly the color of the Wellesford Regal's new gold carpet.

"Darling April, don't ask me, I just got here myself. Diz?" Bascombe hollered. "Where's the Twinkies?"

An intense-looking man of maybe thirty winced and shouted across the room, "Third room back, there's a barrel of junk. But you shouldn't eat that stuff, April. It's no good for you."

"Thanks, love," said the already hefty dancer, forging through the crowd.

"Look at those eyes," Karen murmured in my ear. I didn't see anything unusual about Diz's eyes, except that they were bright enough blue to tell what color they were from fifteen feet off. But I didn't have time to ask if that was what she meant: Bascombe had charged ahead into the next room—where the beer was, except that the sign over the bar called it "bheer." Some of these people had been working on it a while. What's an extra *h* among friends?

"Glad you could come talk to us," Bascombe said, signaling *three* to the bartender as he spoke. "A UFO expert is a little off the track for us. Usually we have well-known fans or writers—"

"Writers?" Karen repeated. "Someone was telling me about discussions?"

"Absolutely." Bascombe turned from the bar and grinned at Karen as he handed her a large paper cup of beer. "Talks and panels, both. And we're giving a fantasy workshop for writers tomorrow afternoon. People can read their stuff and get some feedback—oh, oh."

He was looking at the door to the suite, where the badge checker had stood up in order to listen to a man in an all-too-familiar blue costume. The badge on this one was not pink.

"May I have your attention, please!" the cop yelled. "Please, may I have your attention!"

They quieted faster than most groups would, a wave of silence passing over the crowd. Voices from further back in the suite became distinct and fell silent. "We have had a report of a bomb placed somewhere in the hotel," the cop said. "While it is not likely that there actually is a bomb, we can't take any chances. We must evacuate the hotel immediately."

A murmur started.

"Please exit in an orderly fashion, beginning with those in this room," the cop instructed. "Do *not* return to your rooms. Do *not* use the elevators. The officers in the corridors will direct you. When you reach street level, please keep moving until you have passed the police barricade and your safety can be assured."

"Mack will have kittens," I said in Karen's ear.

"Several," she agreed. "With stripes." She put her cup down on the bar to follow the crowd.

In the next room, the man called Diz pulled a paper cup close to his chest and moved his shoulder as if to protect it from the man who was standing beside him. "Aw, I got time to finish my grape juice," he was saying as we walked past.

"What are you talking about?" his companion demanded, dragging him to his feet by the elbow. "You heard the guy."

"There's time," Diz insisted.

I looked back at him as he pushed a few strands of hair off a balding forehead and combed his fingers down through a straggling beard.

"Take it with you, dammit," the other man said.

Diz reached into his hip pocket for a tissue with which he blotted a few drops from his mustache. The tissue fluttered to the floor, stained purple—a snapshot vision that stayed with me as his friend guided him forward to join the rest of us.

Chapter Three

THE DINGY, ECHOING staircase descended to one end of a
service area, from which an emergency exit opened directly
onto the alley beside the hotel. A long yellow chain
looped between two stanchions kept us from wandering
into the service area, where a couple of canvas trucks were
piled high with dirty linen. The outer door had been
wedged open, and a waiter in a short, silly-looking gold
jacket hurried us through. I thought mournfully of my car,
parked in the barricaded garage under the hotel, and followed along as the straggling double line broke into a half-
run. Another stream of people, from another emergency
exit, joined us as we jogged toward the opening of the
alley.

We emerged onto the street to find wooden barriers
erected halfway down the block, lined with spectators only
a few of whom sported the pink convention badges. Just
ahead of me, as we crossed the street in front of the hotel,
I saw an engineer. I knew he was an engineer because he
held a slab of roast beef folded into a dinner roll in his left
hand. Chewing and frowning, he gained the opposite curb
and turned to look back at the hotel, only to be urged
ahead by some of the SF fans. I knew they were SF fans because no engineer would be caught dead in bearskins. Not
at a conference anyway.

The evacuees rapidly divided into two groups: those who
pressed up to the barricade and stared and those who took
the opportunity to find some other entertainment. Karen
and I enlisted ourselves among the former. The red, blue,

and yellow lights of various emergency vehicles flashed over the building facades and the staring faces, giving the scene as surreal an appearance as any I ever saw on *Star Trek.*

I counted twenty cops standing stiffly in small knots, waiting. Nothing much seemed to be happening. Even the TV news crews just leaned against their vans, bored cameras drooping. What the guy in the helicopter whose *whuppa-whuppa* intermittently echoed among the downtown buildings was doing I couldn't say. Somehow the lack of action was more alarming than the first bald announcement on the top floor of the hotel. My arm circled Karen's shoulders as much for my comfort as for hers.

After a while my heart slipped out of my throat. A few people lost interest and began to leave. Twenty minutes later, with nothing to do but stand around and say an occasional word to my wife, I was ready to leave myself.

"There's Mack," Karen said, for the second time that evening, just as I opened my mouth to suggest going.

Mack stood with his hands in the back pockets of his jeans, inside the barricade, talking to a uniformed officer. The cop nodded, and Mack turned toward us. I shouted his name and waved. He joined us, lounging against the barricade from the inside, and shook his head when Karen asked him what was up. Too busy chewing his mustache to talk.

From the other end of the block, a van slowly made its way through the surging crowd. Three officers, one to drag the wooden horse aside and two to block the crowd, let it into the cleared street. The van pulled up in front of the hotel, and two officers with dogs on leashes got out of the back.

"Sniffers," Mack said.

"What?" Karen asked.

"The dogs. They sniff out explosives. Had to get their

handlers out to bring them here from Nordeast, where the kennels are. That's what took so long." He rocked on his toes, pounding his fist into his left hand, as if waiting to field a baseball. "You guys might as well go home. Two bleeping dogs. Gonna be hours in there. Christ."

"Forrester!" someone called.

I turned to see Dan Bascombe waving at Mack, who motioned to a nearby cop to let him through the barricade. He came over, accompanied by a second man and a slinky blond girl wearing a transparent, flowing sea green robe that left nothing of importance to the imagination. Mack, I noticed, did exactly what I had: fixed his eyes on the maroon felt dragon riding on her right shoulder and tried not to look at anything else.

"What's going on?" Bascombe asked.

"I know about as much as you do," Mack said. "Somebody called the hotel desk and told the clerk a bomb had been planted in some public area of the building. Wouldn't say where, just that they'd better get people out quick."

"Where's Yates?" Bascombe stretched his neck, trying to look over the crowd. "Isn't he supposed to be backing you up?"

"He was helping evacuate. Whatever he did in the army, they sure taught him how to make people move fast and like it." Mack sounded respectful. Yates must be good.

The blond shivered and laid her head on her companion's shoulder. He pulled her close and whispered something into her ear that made her smile. *Cass*, his badge said. The badge had the wide blue stripe of a con-com member across it.

"Did they say this had anything to do with us?" Bascombe asked.

"Not that I know of."

"Any idea who?"

Mack gave him a half-grin that said *forget it*.

"Doesn't finding out come under security?" asked Cass.

His tone was much too bland. I felt Karen shift beside me.

"I contracted for internal security," Mack said. "Not for tapping the phone lines and tracing calls."

"Still, isn't it your responsibility to prevent things like this?" The guy glanced at the blond, who was grinning, and at Bascombe, who was not. "I mean, if we're going to have any security at all, we might as well do it right. Right? What's the point of hassling people with a bunch of rules if the rules don't work?"

"Jeez, Grenzman," Bascombe said through his teeth. "Lay off, will you?"

"Well, seriously, Dan. When the question of hiring outside security first came up last spring, you remember—"

"Can it," Bascombe said.

The blond grinned, lifted her shoulder in a funny little gesture that made her hair catch the light, and took over. "Isn't the whole point of security—well—security?" she asked. "So we can be safe, no matter what?"

Bascombe stared at her face a moment, let his eyes travel down her body and back up again, then turned away.

"I mean," she persisted, adjusting the dragon, "shouldn't a *good* security man find out in advance that something terrible like this was going to happen and prevent it?"

Grenzman, still grinning, lapped his tongue over his upper lip. I felt like socking him.

"What you want is the KGB," Mack remarked. "But I don't think they do private parties." His thumbs were hooked over the front pockets of his jeans. The blond should have been thanking her father for making her a girl.

"No, really—"

"Lay off, Maureen," Bascombe sighed. "Where's your head?"

A shout attracted my attention. Someone in white

kitchen garb confronted a policeman in the middle of the cleared area. Distance and anger made the words incomprehensible, but wild gestures and a stamped foot left no doubt that he thought his place was *in* the hotel, not standing out in the street. A second cop drifted over, and after a few more words the man in white retreated to the other side of the street, stabbing his middle finger into the air, a gesture both officers ignored.

"Let's go home," I said to Karen.

"What about the car?"

"We'll take the bus."

"In that case, let's stop and have something to eat first."

"Hold on," Mack said. "Let me see what this is before you go."

One of the men who had been arguing with the cook had motioned to Mack, who trotted over to him and stood, again with his hands in his back pockets, head cocked, for maybe thirty seconds. When he returned to our little group, he was frowning.

"I don't know about the bomb," he said to Bascombe. "But there was something else. The cops coming out met the Health Department going in."

"Health Department?" Bascombe sounded bewildered.

"Seems somebody called them up and told them the con sells homemade goodies. That's a no-no."

"I know that," Bascombe said, annoyed. "We don't do it, and we don't let the hucksters do it. What an individual fan does, we don't have much control over."

"The hotel is unhappy. Particularly the kitchen crew."

"Dammit, we've got a contract and we can read! You saw the advance program, it says *no food sales* right in with the rest of the policy!"

"You'll have to talk to the environmental people," Mack said.

"We don't sell *any* food," Bascombe insisted. "What we do

distribute is given away, and it's all commercially prepared. Even the popcorn comes prepacked for popping."

"Don't tell me, tell the health officer," Mack said. "Seems there's a story in this morning's paper about an outbreak of hepatitis in Madison, and that's where the goodies in question were home-manufactured." He half-grinned. "The health officer is not happy."

The blond started to giggle. It seemed as good a time as any to leave.

The trusty Route 28 bus carried us home in time for the ten o'clock news, not that the TV told us anything we didn't already know. There was a shot of the police department's bomb disposal robot: a gawky, dark green piece of machinery that had set the city back eighty thousand bucks, as Justin Hugbetter, the late news anchor, informed us four times in a quarter of a minute. A German shepherd that reminded me of Humphrey Bogart gazed blandly into the TV lights while the Channel 7 news team pretended to interview it. The dog gave them five seconds before it yawned at the camera, and the station made a hasty cut away from all those teeth. Hugbetter speculated that the bomb threat had something to do with Palestinian terrorists.

"Or the Irish Republican Army," Karen remarked, yawning as widely as the dog had, but without the sharp teeth. "Where do these guys get their ideas?"

"Looking for someone to thank for their jobs."

"Thank! Maybe it's good news for them, but what about the rest of us?"

"Well, it's not all bad," I said. "The engineers didn't have to listen to much of their speech, and they got their roast beef."

"You and Candide," Karen said. "I suppose you get out of making your speech, too," she added.

"Why? This will be over in a few hours, and my bet is they'll go on just as if it never happened."

I switched channels and discovered that the helicopter had belonged to a news crew. The poor saps were still flying around, broadcasting live, while the guys in the newsroom complained that Mackenzie Forrester was unavailable for comment. They made it sound as if he'd had to hide in a broom closet to get away from them.

"Joe, I'm going with you tomorrow," Karen said, after several minutes of thoughtful silence.

On television the manager of the hotel struggled to conceal his total ignorance of the situation from a badgering reporter.

"I hope so." I yawned. "At least we can sleep late. Poor Mack."

"Poor Mack," Karen said distractedly. "Don't you think about sleeping late, though. We're going to be there absolutely first thing. Where did I put that pamphlet?" She went out to the kitchen and came back with the con schedule. "Nine o'clock there's a panel discussion on breaking into print. That I'd *like* to go to."

"You don't write science fiction," I pointed out.

"Print is print," she shrugged. "I might pick up some pointers, you can never tell."

"What about Joey?"

My wife smiled her I'm-way-ahead-of-you smile. "I talked to Mrs. Eskew when I walked her home. She'll be perfectly happy to come for the morning, too."

I watched a diminutive Darth Vader holding a yellow plastic trash bag stalk through the crowd, collecting empty bheer cups. When he vanished into the female anchor's smile, I reached out and flipped the TV off.

The phone rang at about half past one. I struggled gratefully out of a nightmare lit by a stroboscopic sun in primary colors and rolled over to answer.

37

"Mack," said the phone. "I didn't wake you, did I?"

"You know you did, you s.o.b.," I replied sleepily. "What's up?"

"I thought I'd let you know you still have to get up and talk to these people tomorrow."

"I was figuring on it."

"Good boy," Mack said, with a stab at heartiness. "You want to know what happened?"

"It could have waited for morning."

Talk to the wall.

"We found—I guess I should say the Minneapolis officers found—twenty-four little bomb-type packages."

"Twenty-four!" I could feel the hair rise all over my body. "Twenty-four *bombs*?"

"Bomb-type packages," Mack corrected. He sounded genial. "With four, six-inch what they call utility candles in each, wrapped up in brown paper—skinny little wires sticking out, so on and so forth. All tidily placed where folks could see them if they were looking hard enough. All totally ignored by the dogs. By the time the Bomb Squad got 'em all x-rayed, I think even the robot was pissed. Somebody spent a lot of time on a very expensive joke."

"Candles aren't expensive."

"But cops are. And whoever planted those packages ought to thank the powers that be that those particular dogs had only been trained to sniff explosives."

"I don't get it."

"J.J., sweetheart. There's enough marijuana in this hotel to pay off the Mexican national debt, and some people aren't very shy about it. Imagine the Minneapolis officers coming back with more dogs and a search warrant. Then think what these folks might do to the joker."

"All right, all right, I get the picture," I said.

"Come see me when you get here tomorrow. Meanwhile, do yourself a favor and get some sleep, check?" I heard a yawn.

"I'm gonna log a little sack time myself."

"In the huckster room?" I asked.

"As only about a thousand people know."

"Mack—"

"Sure, I'll take care of myself. You're staying over tomorrow night, check? I've got it fixed on this end. Double room, so if you can arrange it with the Luger lady, Karen can stay, too."

"Thoughtful of you, Mack."

"Yeah." I heard him take a deeper breath than usual. "See you tomorrow, J.J.," he said. "Stay cool."

"Who was that?" Karen murmured as I hung up and rolled over.

"Mack."

"Is he okay?"

"Oh, sure. He just wanted to let me know the party is still on for tomorrow."

For a moment, I thought she might have fallen asleep again, but then she murmured, "He's all heart, Mack is," and hitched the blankets over her ear.

Chapter Four

THE WELLESFORD REGAL was still standing when we arrived on Saturday morning to claim the room Mack had reserved. It takes more than a few packages of candles to bring down the kind of construction that went into hotels in 1916, especially if you don't light them. I didn't check all the crystals in the chandelier on our way up from seeing that our car was still safely in the garage, but at a glance they looked whole. They're probably plastic.

We dropped off my overnight bag—Karen had decided she couldn't hack staying the night—and headed for the action. On the second floor, the registration lines were as long as they had been the day before, but reversed. The walk-ins were now by far the majority. Hardly any were in costume.

"Not fans," Karen diagnosed. "They just want to see where the bomb was."

From the looks of it, she could be right. This group was different from last night's, and not just because of the lack of costume. This crew was mostly male, and they were paying a different kind of attention to the people around them. Something odd about that. . . .

"They look like they're all on the make," Karen said. She sounded puzzled.

Right. Most of the newcomers were guys in their early twenties. They looked a little yuppier than anyone I'd seen yesterday, and they were giving the eye to anything female that came along, not just the cave women and belly dancers.

Mack wasn't checking guns this morning. His place had

been taken by the man named Diz, who, according to his badge, was also a member of the convention committee. With my own plain pink badge pinned to my dress sweatshirt, I cut behind the table to ask him where I could find Mack.

"I think he's in the office," Diz said.

"You don't seem to have much business," Karen remarked.

He blinked up at her with a tentative smile. "No," he agreed. "Hardly anybody has a gun today. That's probably why they shoved this off on me. Somebody must have figured even I could handle it."

He had wound a piece of the plastic tape around his right index finger; after this bitter declaration he squinted along the finger at someone on the other side of the room and emitted a soft "pow." Then, with an almost guilty glance at me, he put his hand down and began to pick at the tape, shoulders hunched. Karen and I moved off.

Mack was in the con office all right, plopped in an overstuffed chair and snoring away. One of the Vulcan twins looked up from a brand-new copy of *Omni* spread on the long table in front of her, licked doughnut icing off her fingers, and asked if she could help us.

"We're friends of Mack's," I said.

"Friends of friends are friends," she said. "We could use some more badgers."

"Badgers?" Karen asked.

The girl, T'Ping—ergo, presumably not Michelle—extended a box of sticky doughnuts toward us. "People to check badges. You must be new to cons?"

"I'm giving a talk," I said.

"Oh, sure, the UFO man." She brushed crumbs of icing off the magazine and turned a page. "Found many?"

"Nary a one."

"Maybe you weren't looking hard enough."

"I don't know how to look any harder." A snore from the chair turned into a snort. Mack yawned and opened his eyes.

"I thought it was you," he said. "What time is it?"

"Twenty to nine. Rise and shine."

"Oof. Do us all a favor and lay off the verse." Mack dragged himself to his feet and yawned again. "I'll be talking to Mr. Jamison in the coffee shop downstairs if anyone wants me, Michelle," he said to the girl.

"I'm Marie."

"Sorry," Mack sighed and led Karen and me into the corridor. "Let's get some coffee. My brain's spinning gears."

We went, not to the free coffee in the con suite, but down the escalator to the Wellesford Regal's pseudoswank breakfast room. Mack asked for a corner booth and ordered the sausage special for one and coffee for three. "Nobody comes here. The service is rotten," he said. "We'll have plenty of privacy."

He was right. I'd thought I might spot an engineer I knew on the way to the restaurant or in it, but we had the place virtually to ourselves. None of the few other customers looked familiar.

"What's up?" I asked.

"Somebody is trying to scuttle this convention," he said. "That bomb scare last night was only part of it. This morning the kitchen crew found their refrigerators standing open and the ovens stuffed with tablecloths. Damn lucky they looked before they lit, or we could have had a fire."

"Good God," Karen exclaimed.

"Hotel's having screaming fits, of course. You'd think their sacred kitchen was my personal responsibility."

"It's not?"

"They hired a couple of rent-a-cops before the con even began," Mack sighed. "After last night's little performance, they hired a couple more to patrol the service areas at night. Anything behind an *Employees Only* sign. That in-

43

cludes kitchens, in my book. Of course," he sighed, "it didn't help any that some clown took the name out of the *Manager On Duty* sign and wrote in 'deceased.' '

I shook my head. "That could have been an engineer," I pointed out. "Typical nerd-type trick. Are you sure this stuff is aimed at the con? What about the engineers, or somebody with a grudge against the hotel?"

"Yeah, could be," Mack said, rubbing his hands upward over his face. "They found a few packs of candles over there, too, now you mention it. Could be I'm just feeling paranoid." The coffee came. He swilled it down and called to the waiter for more. "On the other hand, that call about the food sales was definitely aimed at our convention."

"Do they have to be linked?" Karen asked.

"No, of course not. It's just simpler to have one nut than two, even given a dozen weirdos wandering around in Klingon uniforms. Hey, did you know you're living in the Barony of Nordskogen?"

"The what?"

"Part of the Middle Kingdom." Mack peered, smirking, into his coffee cup, which was still empty. "Okay, no games. Ever heard of the Society for Creative Anachronism?"

"Oh," I said. "Them." Mack looked disappointed. "What have they got to do with Klingons?"

"Nothing, I guess, except they both get dressed up." Mack sighed. "And the Klingons, among others, were playing Killer last night, which reminded me of the other guys and their jousting." He shuddered. "Claymores," he said.

"Last night?"

"No, no." Mack rubbed his eyes. "Christ, I can't take these all-nighters like I used to. We're getting old, J.J."

"What's the Society for Creative Anachronism?" Karen asked.

"Bunch of people who want to resurrect the Middle Ages," I explained.

"Whatever for? I thought we were doing quite nicely with indoor plumbing."

"I don't think they worry about the plumbing. It's the showy parts they resurrect—knights and ladies, jousting matches, storytellers, costumes, jewelry, crafts, medieval cooking."

"I like my microwave," Karen remarked.

"Does she have a romantic bone in her body?" Mack asked me.

"Yes, but the Black Death doesn't appeal to it," Karen told him. "What did you mean, the Klingons were playing Killer?"

"Oh, it's a game," Mack sighed. "They track each other through the hotel and knock each other off. At least the Klingons were playing with laser guns, nothing to worry about." At her frown, he explained, "Laser guns just shoot a beam of light. They don't look like real guns, and these are too weak to hurt anything. Like Laser Tag?"

"What's that?"

"With a male in the first grade, you don't know? Call it Advanced Cops and Robbers. Some teenagers were playing last night. Stick around and take a look later. Anyhow, the Klingon guns don't look real, and they don't go *pow-pow-pow* and scare the mundane guests, like the bunch in camouflage did. One of the concom members was in on that one, for Christ's sake."

"When did they have time to play?" Karen wondered aloud.

"After the bomb search was over. Shit, the night was just getting started. There was even time for the skinny-dipping."

"Skinny-dipping!"

"In the hotel pool. Tradition at SF cons, I'm told," Mack said, barely edging the words past another yawn.

Karen looked at me. "Maybe I should stay tonight, after all," she said.

"I won't swim, don't worry," I said. "I didn't bring my suit."

"J.J., you remember I asked you to keep an eye out for anything interesting?" Mack asked, as Karen punched my arm. "Seen anything?"

"Have you?" I leered.

"Be serious."

"I don't know if I'd know if I did," I told him.

"Yeah, I see what you mean." Mack sighed. "Well, keep your ears open, too. If you get the least little idea something funny's going down, run-do-not-walk to the nearest concom member and tell him, her, or it. We've got some headsets coming in so we can keep in touch." He checked his watch. "Should be here now, in fact. Where is that breakfast? They must be breeding the pig for the sausage."

Karen had glanced at her watch as Mack checked his. "Oh, I'm missing that panel I wanted to hear," she said. "'Scuse me. See you later."

Five minutes after she left, the waiter shuffled over with a platter of sausage, pancakes, and eggs, and plopped it down in front of Mack. He proved himself more awake than he looked by refilling our coffee cups before shuffling away.

"What a rat's nest," Mack said, digging in.

"Your breakfast?"

"No, this job. You wouldn't believe how these guys can argue. See, there's two sides." His hands fell open, one on each side of his plate, almost in appeal. "One of them wants the Gestapo making everybody goosestep at bayonet point, and the other wants a no-holds-barred orgy for everybody, whether they want to participate or not. I'm describing each side from the other one's point of view, check? What it comes down to is about this much difference"—he held his thumb and forefinger maybe a millimenter apart—"in how far you can trust five hundred

46

people, most of whom know at least two dozen of the others and some of whom know just about everybody."

I shrugged.

"The anti-Gestapo is on me for marking the guns, and the anti-orgy is on me for letting people keep them. Among the former we count that jerk Grenzman that was giving me a hard time last night. Among the latter we count the insurance agent." Mack cut into a sausage. "I just hope nobody gets the bright idea of dressing up like a belly-dancer and robbing a bank."

"Not open weekends," I pointed out.

"McDonald's, then. Or this place." He chewed on the sausage. "Cold," he said. "This place they can rob blind, I don't care."

On my way back upstairs, I spotted a large notice board set up between the escalators and the elevators and was bemused to see my own talk on UFOs given a prominent line on the side devoted to T-Con. On the same line—because it was scheduled at the same time—but aimed at the engineers was a much more interesting-looking panel discussion on hardware configurations needed to support a new computer language. Probably I wouldn't understand more than two-thirds of it, but I got onto the escalator feeling disoriented.

Jack Ferraro, scratching his jaw and frowning, was the first person I saw on the second floor. "Hey," he said. "Just the guy I need. Got a few minutes? Or are you getting ready for your talk?"

"Not for nearly three hours."

My stomach was already awash but Ferraro looked worried, and he'd found a blue T-shirt that made a less dazzling combination with the dayglo pink badge, so I could at least look at him. We got into an elevator, largely occupied by a robotlike structure being shepherded by a young kid.

The thing reminded me of R2D2, though larger and not quite so professionally shiny. While I gaped at it, the kid did something at the back, and its eyes, a pair of spotlight bulbs, swiveled, as if focusing on me. Eerie. Ferraro and I crowded as close to the back of the elevator as we could, followed by some yawning Klingons in assorted black and silver uniforms.

"Great robot," one of them said to the kid. "You build it yourself?"

"Nah." The boy looked pleased that someone had thought he might be able to. "Belongs to Mr. Donovan. I'm taking care of it for him."

"Does it run?"

"It's a costume," the kid admitted, obviously braced for the Klingon's disappointment. But the guy got off at the fourth floor with another "great," and the kid was smiling when he wheeled the ersatz robot out on the sixth. By the time we reached the tenth floor, oddly, we had the car to ourselves.

"Everybody still sacked out from last night," Ferraro speculated as we followed the arrows down empty corridors. A slim girl in jeans glanced up from a book that looked like a physics text and nodded us past the door to the con suite. Inside, three guys were already drinking the beer. One of them, I was sure, had been in line to register that morning. It seemed like an odd way to start a convention, to say nothing of a day. I mentioned this to Ferraro.

"Yeah," he agreed. "In fact, that's what I wanted to talk to you about. This con has a funny feel about it."

Shades of Mack, sitting in my family room two months before. I suppressed a shudder and asked, "What do you mean?" while I stirred whitener into coffee from the urn set up in the first room of the suite. Ferraro headed for a table.

"I'm not sure," Ferraro said, settling himself. "Cons are . . . a different kind of place. A safe place. Look at the costumes you see. Where else could you wear them in public? Not many places. Especially the ones that are nothing but body paint, though you won't see those in Minnesota. Nobody puts you down for being your own eccentric self. You read me? But there's an, I dunno, an insecurity about this con."

"I don't get you."

Ferraro's shoulders twitched. "Just a feeling." He jerked his head toward the second room, where the three guys were drinking. "That's part of it. They don't look like fans. They don't even look like fake-fans. They look more like fraternity types, you know what I mean? Fans don't wear little alligators to cons. So what are these guys doing here?"

"What's the difference between them and fake-fans?"

"Fake-fans don't give a damn about science fiction either, but it's not the same. Maybe they only come to party, but you've met them before."

The gold-clad belly dancer stopped to talk to the girl checking badges across the room. She noticed Jack and me, waggled her fingers at us, smiled, and waddled off in search of a Twinkie fix.

"That's April Thorney," Jack said. "I've talked to her a lot at other cons. Interesting woman, very bright. Everybody likes April. She's kind of a mother figure, you know? She *belongs* here. Those guys in the other room I've never seen in my life, and I have a good head for faces. After all, I'm basically a salesman in the mundane world."

Ferraro owns his own business. Nowadays he hires people to do his selling for him, but I saw his point. "Then there's other things," he continued. "Donovan, of all people, asking if anybody's got a gun."

"I think that's—"

"Hey!" shouted an outraged female voice in the second room. Somebody mumbled something. I heard cloth rip, followed a second later by the crack of a slap. April Thorney, her doughy skin flushed scarlet, lumbered past us clutching the front of her costume together. Jack stood up fast, knocking his chair to the floor. I was a little slower.

"That's it," the bartender shouted. "You've had enough. Out you go."

The girl checking badges faced her open book down on the tall stool and strode across the room. She was half the size of April Thorney, not much over five feet tall and not much over a hundred pounds. Ferraro, closer to the inner door than I was, hurried toward her.

"Free beer all weekend," one of the drinkers shouted.

"Have you for false a'vertisement," added one of the others. " 'N' you can't even spell."

The badger stood in the doorway with her hands on her hips. "Okay, what's going on?" she demanded.

"Now, she's more like it," one of the drunks cooed. "Not as sloppy fat."

The girl blinked.

"Free beer is free beer," the first drunk declared, slapping the bar. "I want my beer."

"You've had enough," the bartender insisted. He looked about fifteen, though he must have been at least nineteen to be serving beer, and he looked scared.

"You don't give it to me, pizza-face, I'm gonna take it."

"Out you go," said the girl, jerking her thumb.

"Girls," said the third drunk. "Where're the rest of the girls? S'posed to be lotsa girls."

"That one ripped April's bra," the bartender said to Jack, who had sidled past the badger into the room. "Can you believe it? Reached out and grabbed it and ripped it in two! What kind of jackass does something like that to somebody's costume?"

"Who're you calling a jackass?" the drunk demanded. The bartender backed up, sidestepping to get behind the beer keg. I followed Jack into the inner room, my stomach protesting that it belonged to anybody but a hero.

Three of them. Three of us. And the girl, who quietly stepped one foot back and waited, balanced, still blocking the door. With a jolt I realized that it was one of the Vulcan twins.

"Call security, Willard," she said.

Out of our sight, in the third room of the suite, a door closed softly. A moment later the bomb went off.

Chapter Five

FIRECRACKERS WERE STILL snapping a full minute later. Mack inexplicably charged through the door of the con suite as the last two banged. The acrid smoke of gunpowder stopped him at the door of the third room.

The three drunks had disappeared.

Mack started to laugh.

Ferraro and I looked at each other. Him holding his nose and me holding my breath, we shoved our heads past Mack for a look. Scattered around the room were dozens of huge paper flowers, sprung open by the tiny firecrackers.

"Holy buckets," Ferraro said. He stood looking at the room very soberly for ten or twelve seconds, then started to giggle. The bartender fetched himself out from behind the keg and came to look over my shoulder.

"I don't see what's so funny," he said.

"You probably got a decent night's sleep," Mack remarked. "We'd better make sure there aren't any sparks still going."

The girl returned—I wasn't sure when she'd left—and began sifting through the brightly colored paper. "I didn't see anybody in the hall," she said.

Ferraro stepped into the room and bent to pick up a bright orange flower. "I haven't seen these since fireworks were still legal! I must have been a little kid," he said, his voice still high with laughter. "Where do you think they got them? Wisconsin?"

"What happened?" Mack asked the girl.

"We had some ugly drunks we were going to toss out,"

she said. "I heard somebody leave this room through that other door, and then the firecrackers started. I ran out to see if I could catch him, but whoever it was had already gone."

"Service access at the end of this corridor," Mack said, nodding. "Probably hightailed it through that door and down the stairs and back into the public corridors next floor down. Maybe one of the hotel people saw him. Good thinking, Marie."

"I'm Michelle."

"Sorry." Mack shoved his hands into his back jeans pockets, his lower lip sticking out as he stared at the mess. Ferraro and I, Michelle, and the bartender had all the flowers picked up. We'd uncovered a stained metal tray on which the fuse must have been lit; the solid twist carpet the Wellesford Regal had installed everywhere above ground floor showed no signs of smoldering. "I wonder if this is the same joker we had yesterday," Mack mused, "or just some other inspired mother—uh—fellow."

The girl laughed. From the first room somebody yelled, "Hey, isn't anybody badging?" and she hurried back to her post.

"What about these drunks?" Mack asked the bartender. "That's what I came for. We got a call from a Miss Thorney."

"I bet you did," Ferraro muttered.

"I don't know about those guys." The bartender cleared his throat. "They walked in maybe half an hour ago and chugged about four beers apiece. I was telling them it was time to slow down when April came by and one of them grabbed her. She told him to get lost, and he ripped the top of her costume." The kid started picking nervously at a spot on his left cheek. "Right down the front." He gave Mack a quick, half-shamed sideways glance. "Man, does April have a lot to spill! Anyway, she went running out of

54

here, and I told those guys no more beer. Then *these* two guys and Michelle came in, and in the middle of that there was a *pow*! and it started sounding like World War Three in here."

"Did you hear somebody leave from this room, too?"

"Yeah, but I don't know who it could have been. I didn't see anybody in there when I was picking up empty cups before, and that door only opens from the inside."

Mack, with a glance at the hydraulic closer at the top of the door, went over and opened it with three stiffened fingers. He tried the outer knob the same awkward way. It resisted. Carefully, he eased the door closed with his toe so that it was only half an inch ajar. It pushed itself shut. The latch clicked solidly. "Huh," he said. "Got a buck, J.J.?"

I pulled a dollar out of my wallet and handed it over. Mack opened the door in the same stiff-fingered way, slipped the folded bill between latch and frame, and eased the door shut. No click.

"Run out and see if you can push it open, check?" he said to me. "Don't leave any prints. If it opens, you get your buck back."

"Thanks," I said, on my way. I put my shoulder to the outside of the door and got my dollar back.

"Didn't you spoil the fingerprints?" the bartender asked Mack.

"I doubt there were any," he said. "But if there were, do you open doors the way I just did?"

"No, I grab the handle like—"

"Uh-uh," Mack cautioned. "That's right. I can take prints, just in case anybody ever wants to match 'em up, but personally, I think it's a waste of time."

"Can't you figure out from the prints who did it?"

"No."

"I thought—"

"You thought half the American populace had their

prints on file with the FBI. They don't, and even if they did, you can't just go through the file and find somebody cold like that. You have to have maybe a dozen possibles at most. *Then*, if you're lucky, you make your ID."

"No, I thought the Minneapolis cops had a computer."

Mack glanced at the kid, a professional-looking glance. "Yeah, but the chance of a cold hit here is just about zip, unless our joker is also a felon. I can entertain the city if you want, but I charge extra for making an ass of myself."

"Oh." The bartender flushed.

"Who's been in here this morning, do you remember?"

"Gosh, no." The boy looked relieved. "Must have been fifty people, though it's not so busy now. The whole concom's been here, and one of the rent-a-cops promoted himself a doughnut and coffee. But the rest of them ... I could give you maybe a name or two, but that's all."

"That's already more than a dozen, isn't it?" Mack pointed out.

The bartender, cowed, retreated behind the bar as two more of the golden-boy types showed up demanding free beer. "That I don't like," Mack said, nodding at the new-comers.

He got a Styrofoam cup from a stack by the coffee machine and jammed it over the doorknob, wrote *Do not touch* on it with a thin-line marker, and retreated with a thoughtful glance at the two drinkers. Our stone cold coffee still stood where Ferraro and I had left it. I got the bartender to pour mine into his sink, but Jack drank his down in five swallows.

"See what I mean?" he said. "Guys like that don't belong. Izods and Reeboks and the hair to go with them."

"I guess. Between drunks and bomb scares and people calling the Health Department—"

"Health Department?" Ferraro interrupted. He blinked at me. "Someone called the Health Department?"

56

"So I hear."

"And complained that people were selling food that might be contaminated?"

I nodded. "Something like that. There was a story in yesterday's newspaper about a hepatitis outbreak. They linked it to that."

"That's interesting," Ferraro remarked. His eyes narrowed as he stared into space. "Same thing happened a few years ago to another con. . . ." He looked back at the two guys drinking beer. "And them." He gnawed on one knuckle for a moment. "No, it can't be. Somebody's doing a copycat. I bet—" He broke off as three more prep-school types came through the con suite door. "Where'd you see the announcement?" he asked one of them.

"Somebody put a flyer in the frat house mailbox," the kid said, grinning. "Great, isn't it? Didja get a load of how some of these weirdos are dressed?"

"It takes some imagination and ingenuity," Ferraro said coldly, and beckoned me out with his head. "We'll have to find Dan Bascombe," he said. "And where did Forrester go?"

"Probably back to the office."

"Let's go."

We rode down in the elevator with a skinny old woman who had a stuffed black cat slung over her shoulder. At least, I thought it was stuffed. Then the elevator halted and the cat lifted its head, looked straight into my eyes, and yawned.

Bascombe was now the weapons checker. I left Ferraro expounding his theory and went looking for Karen, whose panel discussion should have broken up. I didn't have far to look. She was sitting on one of the benches near the far wall of the central area, scribbling in her notebook.

"Just a minute," she said, without glancing up. "I want to

get this idea down before I lose it."

I'm used to Karen's scribbling by now. I brushed a few palm fronds out of the way and plopped onto the bench next to her. She was using her special semi-shorthand. I can't read it, but it was full of the long dashes she uses for quotation marks, so I realized she must be recording a conversation. From the length of it, something ongoing.

People were standing behind me, talking. I tuned in just in time to hear a man's voice—familiar sounding, but I couldn't place it—say, "It's old friends like you that I worry about. I don't know what she might be saying to them. You know what she's like." The reply, a murmur, sounded female and vaguely comforting.

"You think I should?" the man said.

The female voice murmured a few more words.

"That'd be great." After a moment Karen stopped scribbling.

" 'I don't know what she might be saying to them,' " she quoted. "There's a capsule story right there, isn't there?"

"Shhh."

"Don't worry, they're gone." Karen grinned at me. "I still have a few manners."

I glanced behind me and saw only a woman examining a panel discussions schedule posted beside the door of one of the small meeting rooms a good ten feet away.

"Could she—" I whispered.

"No. They're over by the elevators," Karen assured me. "See that woman in the denim muumuu? With the white turtleneck under it? Her and the guy with her."

The woman was April Thorney, changed out of her ruined costume. The man with her looked familiar, too. He half-turned, tugging at his mustache, and I saw that it was the man who had helped Mack check weapons the evening before. "I hope they didn't figure out what you were doing," I muttered. "That guy's on the concom."

58

"Really?"

"He's the one helping Mack coordinate the security arrangements."

"Ooof," Karen said.

Bascombe, I saw, was standing behind the weapons-check table, leaning forward onto his fingers. Ferraro, still with him, turned to look toward the elevators.

"Hey, Yates!" Bascombe yelled, but Yates was already stepping into the elevator. The doors slid shut behind him.

The concom chair reached under the table and came up with a two-way radio, into which he spoke. Ferraro waved a two-fingered salute at him and ambled away.

"Joe? Let's go to the huckster room," Karen said, studying the map of the con on the program. "I want to see what's for sale."

Curious as I was about what Bascombe and Ferraro had discussed, it really was none of my business. I figured that if it was important, Bascombe would tell Mack all about it.

"Okay," I said, and let Karen lead the way to the hucksters.

Books. Books, books, books, and more books. Books new, books used, books stiff and shining, books ancient and disheveled and turning yellow. Old magazines—things with titles like *Galaxy* and *Astounding Science Fiction* and *Amazing* and *Fantastic* and *Thrilling Wonder*. Very expensive, that last one, shrink-packed in clear plastic and displayed under glass. But even if you had no taste at all for science fiction, you could have spent hours looking at the other things for sale. Jewelry, both tawdry and beautiful—Karen bought herself a silver pin, a lacy butterfly with an oval slice of reddish brown agate in one wing—pottery, wood carving, drawings and sculptures of strange creatures and stranger fantasies, plastic laser guns like the one I'd seen the day before, buttons. I bought a large button that asked *Where do you get your ideas?* and ceremoniously pinned it to Karen's shirt, and she reciprocated with one that advised *Don't panic, it's only ones and zeros.* Banners, posters, several sizes of dragons, like the one the blond had been wearing, in a bizarre assortment of colors, doodads to hold up your hair, doodads to hang from your belt, belts to hang doodads from, and—claymores. At the sight of them, my hair tried to hold itself up, unaided.

The room was thronged with fans in a buying mood and with hucksters cheerfully selling. At the sword display near one back corner of the room I spotted the guy who had given Mack such a hard time the night before, Cass Grenzman. He was lovingly, repeatedly, running his left index finger along the oriental-looking carvings in a snakelike blade, glancing up occasionally to talk to the dealer as he leaned on the table. Other equally ornate knives lay jewel-like on a heavy, blood red velvet cloth that hung to the floor in front of the display. I shuddered and turned away.

T'Ping-Marie—or, possibly, T'Pong-Michelle— sauntered past with a Vulcan salute, which I tried to return without success.

Karen's smile suggested that the incident would go down in her notebook at the first opportunity. Others whose faces or costumes I recognized ambled along with the crowd.

Somebody was twitting one of the Darth Vaders about his television appearance. He responded with an indignant, "Hell, somebody had to do it."

April Thorney, with the advice of Diz Donovan, smiled as she chose a pair of carved chopsticks to pin up her dark hair. And the guy who'd been checking badges at the con suite door the night before dickered with one of the booksellers over a yellowed paperback. A little more of this, I thought, and I could feel right at home. I was forking over three bucks for an only slightly used copy of Ursula LeGuin's *The Language of the Night*, something Karen had heard highly recommended at the panel discussion she'd attended, when a hand landed on my shoulder.

"Glad to see you," Dan Bascombe said. "You're ready for your one o'clock, aren't you? It'll be in room D, right next door."

"Thanks," I said. "I was going to check on that after we got done buying out the place."

Bascombe shook his head. "Too late by then," he said, grinning. "Say, you got a minute? I'd like to ask you a couple of questions."

"Sure."

"Let's get out of this crowd."

I promised Karen I'd be right back. Bascombe led me out of the huckster room and across the central area to the corridor leading to the smaller meeting rooms. A badger at the door of a darkened room nodded at us as we passed. Inside, I glimpsed a screen showing a movie I didn't recognize.

"Ah," Bascombe said.

A tall, slender, bearded man was walking toward us, head down and hands clasped pensively behind him. He looked up at Bascombe's voice and said hello.

"Pete, I want you to hear something," Bascombe said. "Got a minute or two?"

Pete, whose badge said he was a baron, nodded and turned on his heel to join us. "Here will do," Bascombe said. He stepped into an empty room, switching on the lights. "This is Joseph Jamison," he said to the baron.

"Oh, the UFO man."

"Right. Listen, we've got something going on here. Have you been around this morning?"

"No, I just got up."

"That bomb business last night?" Bascombe said. "That was for us."

Pete raised a skeptical eyebrow. "Come on, Dan, aren't you being a little paranoid?"

"Nope." Bascombe stuck his hands in his pockets and took a deep breath. "We've had the Health Department here."

"Oh?" The baron suddenly looked interested.

"Asking about homemade food, as you've probably guessed. This time it was linked to a story in the newspaper. That's point one. Point two, somebody set off some little firecrackers in the con suite—that's what I wanted to check with you, J.J. Something I never saw before. They make paper flowers come out somehow."

"Where would they get those?" Pete asked.

"Hell, I don't know. Wisconsin, maybe, or whichever Dakota they sell fireworks in. Maybe they're left over from the Fourth of July. Listen. I took over the weapons check so Diz could take a pee and grab some grape juice, and guess what? We've got a lot of college boys registering this morning."

"Fraternity types?"

Bascombe nodded. "One of them gave April Thorney a bad time about her costume. Drunk. I think we're in for trouble." He glanced at me, as if checking his facts, and I nodded.

"You're wondering if the guy pulling tricks is the same guy who gave the SCA such a hard time last winter." Baron Pete ran his tongue over his teeth. "I dunno, Dan, we never proved anything."

"Who did you think it was?"

I got a mistrustful glance. "Certain guy we gently suggested ought to give sword fights a miss, because people were getting hurt when he fought them. The first few bruises we sort of took in stride, but then he broke somebody's arm. It looked deliberate, and he'd been arguing with the guy just that morning. So that did it. Both

62

ways. We told him we didn't want him fighting and he decided to leave us, with a few interesting words to describe people who join the SCA." He glanced at me again and said to Bascombe, "You know who. We told him he'd be better off in the Dark Horde, and so far as I know that's where he went."

Bascombe nodded again. "Thanks." He turned to me. "You're probably pretty confused. The SCA is the Society for Creative Anachronism, and Pete's the local seneschal—president, that is."

"I was on my way to figuring that out," I said. "I've heard of the SCA, but I didn't know what the name of the office was."

The baron grinned. "One of our members is researching UFOs in medieval times. You know, the Romans saw what they called flying shields, something like our saucers. This guy thinks some of the visions the crusaders had were UFOs. You ought to talk to him."

"I'd like to," I lied. Ten to one the guy was what I call a fan and Ferraro calls a ufonut, somebody who's out of his head when it comes to UFOs. I'd had them accuse me of manufacturing evidence that showed a hoax had occurred, or—worse, really—taking the same evidence as proof that a saucer had landed.

"He'll probably be in your audience," the baron said. "That all you wanted, Dan? Because I'm starving. I was on my way up for some doughnuts."

"You're in luck," Bascombe said, with a comradely slap for the baron's shoulder. "I sent somebody on a doughnut run twenty minutes ago. They should be back by now."

The baron left. Bascombe, lips compressed, clapped his hands once, startling me. "Cass Grenzman," he said. He glanced at me. "That's the guy the SCA tossed out, though they're too nice to describe it that way. He's given me nothing but trouble over this con for damn near a year. I should have guessed. What does he have to lose?" Bascombe shook his head. "Not money. He's not in with the shirt off his back, like some of us. You wouldn't catch him taking an equity loan on his house—if he had one."

"Seems to me the thing to do is to find out where he was when the fuse to those firecrackers was lit," I said.

"I can tell you where he'll say he was," Bascombe sighed. "In our lovely friend Miss Tesla's bed."

Chapter Six

"DAN?" THE BADGER from the film room poked his head in at the door. "Could you come here a minute?"

"Sure."

We followed the badger back to the darkened room, where the girl in charge of the video projector greeted us with visible relief. "Outside," she said, slipping out of the darkened room with a furtive motion. She carried a grease-stained box that had held doughnuts.

"Look at this," she said, when we had put five yards between us and the door of the movie room. She lifted the lid of the box, after checking over her shoulder. "I found them when I was looking for the tape of *TRON*."

Bascombe reached into the box and pulled out a videotape cartridge. "*Bizarre Sex Wars*," he read from the label. "What is this? Good lord, *Sex Kittens Go to College*? And—" His ears reddened. "I'm not touching that. Where did you say they were?"

"In the case," the girl said, now blushing herself. "Where the tapes of the other movies are. I got the schedule mixed up and I thought I should be showing *TRON*, so I went looking for the tape. The right tapes were out on the table where they should have been, so I didn't really have to be looking for anything. *TRON's* tomorrow, same time."

"I'll take these. Is this all of the, uh, unusual ones?"

She nodded.

"Thanks." The girl shrugged and returned to the darkened room. "We don't even show anything rated R, let

65

alone X," Bascombe said. "I think that kid's about fourteen. Volunteer. Damn. I know her father! When I get my hands on this jerk—" He shook his head, shoulders hunched. "When do you think the vice squad is programmed to pounce? Jeez, where am I gonna ditch these things?"

"Anywhere," I suggested.

"I ought to call Forrester." He remembered that he'd left his two-way radio buried beneath the screaming-purple Ping-Pong balls in the box under the table where he'd been checking weapons. "I'll stick these in there, for the time being," he decided, fists tight. "I need the radio. Good excuse to go into the box."

I walked as far as the check-in desk with him, nodded to Donovan, and then went on to the huckster room, where I almost collided with Cass Grenzman on my way in. He shoved past me with neither a sign of recognition nor an apology, breathing hard.

I found Karen chatting with a rangy, dark-haired man who was lounging, feet up, behind a long table loaded with old magazines. A couple of people half the age of the magazines—'zines, in con talk—browsed along the display.

"Oh, here he is," Karen said, catching sight of me. "Joe, this is Frank Pawlicky."

The huckster's feet came down, and he lurched forward with a friendly grin, right hand out. "Nice to meet you, Jamison," he said. "I've read some of your investigation reports. Good stuff."

"Thanks," I said, surprised.

I'd thought an SF fan might be disappointed at my work. After eleven years of checking out about eighty percent of the sightings in three states in the upper Midwest, the score was me fifty-seven, insufficient evidence two, saucers zero. And here this guy was going on about assessing concrete evidence and the ghastly state of public education.

"Kids don't learn to think is the trouble," he declared. "I often think the only way they ever learn rational argument is by reading SF. Not that sword-and-sorcery junk, which can muck up a mind as fast as any third-grade teacher."

One of the browsers gave him a startled glance and moved off.

"Lost a customer," Pawlicky commented genially. "That's okay. That kind I don't need."

He was getting up steam for another assault on modern education when the sleek blond of the night before turned up, somewhat more opaquely dressed in jeans and a loose shirt. "Hi, Frank," she said. "You seen Cass this morning?"

"He was looking at knives a while ago."

"Here? In this room?" The blond's eyebrows rose.

"Yeah, over there." Frank's loose wave included a quarter of the room, but the blond turned accurately and stared at the table of swords only about twenty feet away but barely visible through the crowd.

"He didn't stop to say hello to me," she said.

"Maybe he's working his way around the room," Frank suggested. "He was talking to Sue Evers before that."

"Was he!" said the blond, in a tone that made me glad I wasn't Cass Grenzman, or Sue Evers, for that matter.

"Con business most likely," Frank said. He sounded placating, and a bit nervous.

The blond gave him a stiff little nod and moved on, her mouth set.

Karen, examining the schedule, had found another panel going on that she wanted to sit in on. "I've missed five minutes," she said, "but it's out at eleven thirty. We'll have time for lunch before you start talking."

We agreed to meet at the top of the escalator at eleven thirty-five, and Karen hurried away, groping for her notebook in her purse. Frank was already talking about UFOs and the state of mathematics education in Minnesota. He was obviously a one-topic man who'd found a thousand ways to lead into it. With nothing better to do but work up a case of stage fright, and with Joey just starting first grade, I leaned my elbow on a box of 'fifties *Galaxy* and listened.

I frittered the rest of the morning away, eyes and ears dutifully open. For a while, I was a mostly silent fourth in a technical conversation on the topic of growing tomatoes. The sight of April Thorney and the blond, deep in conversation on the other side of the room, caught my eye. Ferraro had probably been accurate in calling April a mother figure. They were too far away to hear, but the blond's gestures were choppy, short, almost violent, while April's were slow and soothing. After a moment she put her hand on the blond's elbow, and they stepped onto the elevator. I discovered the topic of the now-passionate discussion on whose fringe I lingered: zucchini.

Mack had his own problems, I observed when I glanced into the office. He'd finally had to station a couple of his volunteers in the lobby to keep the more high-spirited fans from shocking the stodgier engineers into insanity—to say nothing of the middle-aged double-knit ladies who came for the Wellesford Regal's salad bar lunch.

Nevertheless, complaints kept rolling in. The morning manager, a grim woman who looked as if she could have handled last night's TV reporters in a way they'd never forget, rumbled through the reception area and into the con office like a late-season thunderstorm, leaving Bascombe fluttery and Mack with his brows an inch higher than usual. I caught the end of the performance and, exhibiting more common sense than I'm known for, removed myself from the scene of action.

Karen and I went out to Arby's for lunch. She was wide-eyed and chattery, full of news about writing and writers.

No help to my frazzling nerves. This wasn't the first time I'd talked to a group about UFOs, but all the same I found the idea of getting up on a speaker's platform and mouthing off a little daunting.

Bascombe, bless him, was on hand at one o'clock to introduce me to my audience of maybe four dozen people, counting Karen, ranging in age from about fourteen to at least seventy, not one of them in costume. Scanning the group from the dais while the concom chair talked, I recognised Yates, sitting in a get-away seat on the end of the third row, and right behind him the man who had been talking to Diz Donovan when the evacuation began the night before. Ah, yes, and there was Ferraro, solidly in the middle of the audience and sporting an encouraging smile. I wondered which of the rest was the medievalist. Bascombe cracked the obligatory jokes about small green humanoids and got the obligatory titters, but, to be fair, he kept it short.

Public speaking is not my bag, especially when I'm perched on a platform and fenced off from the audience by a long table. When Bascombe excused himself, pleading other duties and turning on a tape recorder in order, he said, to miss nothing, I came out from behind the table, sat on the edge of it, and picked up the microphone. Informality I'm almost good at. It helped that I knocked the blue skirt loose from the edge of the table and had to fumble with the Velcro strip that held it on to reattach it. Helped the informality, I mean—not me.

I gave them the full treatment, starting with what's needed for scientific evidence. Most UFO sightings are honest mistakes. A little over a year ago, I reminded them, a weather balloon glowing in the late afternoon sunlight had made a lot of people in the Twin Cities stand up and take notice. Enough of the notice-takers had been driving east on I-94 to cause a major traffic snarl. Other sightings are illusions or outright hallucinations. It's amazing, I said, how often the little green men choose to befriend people who have recently established a close relationship with a controlled substance. I saw Yates frown and nod at that.

Then there are the hoaxes, infrequent but to me the most intriguing. The creative imagination of the American public is grossly underrated. I once encountered a bright nine-year-old who had a town of ten thousand souls locking their doors and fearfully scanning the winter sky with the help of only three extra-large Mylar balloons and a mail-order canister of helium.

All of this I discussed on autopilot. People would wander in and stand for a few minutes in the back of the room, arms folded and mouths pinched while they decided whether it was worth staying or not, and most of them would wander out. Like as not, if they decided to stay, they'd meander down to the front few rows and hitch sideways to an empty seat. Once in a while somebody who had been in the audience from the beginning would stand up and stroll out. Still, part of the audience was as predictable as sunshine in the Sahara.

As for instance, the medievalist. When I asked for questions, sure enough, he stood and pronounced his theory about crusaders' visions. I let him go on for a while; when even the loyal core of the audience began shifting and talking to each other I pled ignorance and called for more questions.

"You haven't talked about the electromagnetic effects of UFOs," said a fat guy in a plaid shirt and a beard. "How can an illusion or, for that matter, a weather balloon, cause disruptions to a car's ignition system?"

"I have several theories about that," I said. In the back of the room, Karen smiled and nodded. "First, I think we can actually trace the stories about so-called electromag-

70

netic disturbances back to a first case. I strongly suspect that once the idea reached the public, it appealed to a lot of people who had some time missing that they didn't want to account for, say, to their wives."

A murmur of laughter at that. "But what caused that first case?" the man asked, dogged as any other nut.

"Artistic imagination." Ferraro grinned. He knew what was coming. "Guy named Newman published a novel called *The Flying Saucers* in, I think, nineteen fifty, that talked about effects on car ignitions. A lot of people agree that was the first mention of the phenomenon." I raised my eyebrows at the man, who nodded grudgingly, and went on. "Apart from outright hoax and the occasional all-too-real psychotic delusion, in many cases there is strong evidence that the car in question had a faulty electrical system. Most of these cases happen at night, particularly when there's been a heavy dew, suggesting some sort of electrical short. We've already talked about the variety of objects in the night skies people can mistake for UFOs. If, by coincidence, one of these objects was in view at the time the car stalled—"

"You attribute the electromagnetic effects of UFOs to coincidence, then?" the man asked.

"In some cases. Imagine what people would think if, right now, somebody released a balloon from the hotel roof and someone in the street mistook it for a UFO and the lights went out—"

The lights went out.

After a moment of silence I heard myself mutter, "Oh, for Christ's sake."

The words seemed to release a stir of words and motion. One of the folding chairs clattered to the floor. A draft touched the nape of my neck. Suddenly, I wished I had my back to the wall.

"I think we'd better just sit tight," I said, my voice

shrunken by the sudden absence of the sound system. I repeated the words, louder.

From the larger room beyond, there came a babble of complaint. Someone shouted, "All right, just take it easy and stay where you are. We're trying to find out what went wrong, and we'll have the lights back just as fast as we can."

Most of the people in my smaller room weren't sitting tight; I heard muffled protests as some started to grope their way past others toward the door. Setting down the microphone, I managed to knock over my water glass, which rolled to the platform and crashed.

"Please sit still," I said, louder. "That was just me being a klutz." The black was the black of a coal pit, except for the dim red exit signs over the doors: all the meeting rooms were in the core of the hotel, cut off from windows. As my eyes adjusted to the dark, I discovered that the door of the room was faintly visible, a tall rectangle grayed with the light that came up the escalator into the central hall. Silhouettes moved in the doorway from time to time—most of them going out, a few coming in.

"We'll suffocate!" said an anguished voice.

"No, we won't," I said. "Hear the fans?"

I hadn't realized until I spoke that I had been listening for the whisper of the ventilation system. I felt my scalp begin to relax. If the fans were on, the power failure couldn't be general.

Elevator doors whooshed open. Light spilled across the floor beyond the door. "What's going on?" somebody asked.

"It must be just this floor," a woman close to the speaker's table remarked.

"What *about* the electromagnetic effects of UFOs?" my questioner demanded.

"Damned if I know," I said. Out in the larger room, the same voice called again for calm. My lunch declared that it didn't care about ventilation and began to argue with my stomach.

A hundred years or so later, when the lights came on, I found I still had nearly fifteen minutes of my hour to fill. Over half my audience had vanished in the dark, presumably to a better world of their own choosing, without the assistance of any little green men. Karen was still there, of course, and at least Ferraro had stuck with me. So had Yates, now standing near the wall, where I guessed he'd ended up after making sure no one got himself hurt. Donovan's friend was gone. Yates gave me a victory sign and walked back to his seat.

"The power failure was just on this floor," said a woman in an elegant sapphire blue velvet gown.

"Do you know what happened?" I asked.

"No, but apparently it wasn't anything serious," she said. She settled a few pins that were creeping out of an elaborate knot of red hair on top of her head as she swept down the aisle and sat down. "Are you still talking about UFOs?"

Her badge was striped with blue: concom. The capacity of these people to go about their business after the most outrageous interruptions astonished me.

"I guess so," I said.

"Carry on, by all means."

Not that I expected many more questions: my audience dwindled by the second.

"If you hear that a UFO was spotted over the hotel just as the lights went out, what will you think?" demanded Plaid Shirt.

"I'll think you set it up."

At the back of the shrunken audience my wife shook her head and frowned. *Getting testy, Joe,* I could almost hear her say.

* * *

Karen came forward to meet me as all but the last two or three hangers-on left the room. I'd have been stuck arguing my evidence for some of the hoaxes I'd uncovered for the rest of the afternoon, but the woman in the blue velvet dress announced that the room was needed for another meeting and firmly shooed the stragglers out.

"Good speech," Karen said. "How'd you arrange the business with the lights?"

"Come on."

She mock-shivered. "Scary, for a few seconds there. Let's go up to the con suite. I said I'd meet a couple of other writers after you were done talking."

"Do you write?" asked the woman in the blue dress.

I peered at her badge. So that was Sue Evers! No wonder Grenzman had stopped to talk to her.

She smiled at Karen. "A lot of fans write."

We left Plaid Shirt arguing with the medievalist and collected Ferraro on the way out of the meeting room. The central area was even more crowded than I'd seen it before, although registration would close in only an hour. Everywhere, the topic of conversation was the power failure. Half of those who had endured it were busily exaggerating the eeriness to those who'd had the misfortune to be on another floor at the time, while others speculated on the cause. Ferraro, on the point of joining us in the con suite, stopped to talk to a friend and signaled that he'd join us later. Karen and I found we had an elevator to ourselves.

"I'm glad I came," she said, punching the button for the tenth floor. "I'm learning a lot of interesting stuff about the business end of writing. It'll take days to digest it all."

"Great," I said, giving her a sideways hug as the elevator slowed for the fourth floor. I was still grinning down at her when the doors slid open.

"Don't trust him. Not even an inch." The blond-of-the-sea-green-dress, still in jeans and a sloppy shirt, but now with her face blotched pink around her eyes and nose, stepped into the car and pounded the sixth-floor button with the side of her fist. "Not one inch," she repeated, turning to face the doors with both fists still clenched. The car slowed and the doors slid open and she dashed out. I looked after her with my jaw hanging.

"Wasn't that the girl in the Frederick's of Hollywood outfit?" Karen asked. "Out in the street last night?"

"Yes," I said. "Don't you remember? She was in the huckster room before lunch talking to that magazine dealer."

"Is that who it was? I was looking at the program and I didn't pay any attention."

"She seemed okay then."

Karen's mouth twitched in a crooked little smile. "Times have changed, it would seem," she said.

She probably caught up with Cass Grenzman, and he didn't give a damn, I thought. But Karen could figure that out for herself.

The elevator stopped to let on people at each floor after that. At last, packed into the car as tightly as wires in a computer cable, we arrived at the tenth floor. No longer deserted, the con suite was buzzing with the news of the second-floor power failure. Karen spotted the people she had promised to meet and stepped forward, waving.

Mack spotted me.

Chapter Seven

"I GOT TO talk to you," Mack said, looking at the crowd and not at me.

"Sure."

I excused myself from Karen and followed Mack into the hall and through the *Employees Only* door to the service corridor, a narrow passage painted a depressing green and floored with dirty gray tile. Mack had his cop walk back, arms swinging wide to accommodate an invisible gun in an invisible holster slung at his side, chest lifted under an invisible badge. I know trouble when I see it.

"Where were you when the lights went out?" he asked.

"Down in the cellar—"

"Eating sauerkraut," he finished with me. "No joke, J.J., we've got a bad one. Somebody swiped a blade from that dealer in the huckster room when the dark came down."

"I can see the temptation," I said. "Some of the knives he's got on display are real works of art."

Mack blew a deep breath up his face and folded his arms. "This one was not on display."

I cocked my head at him.

"There were twelve knives in a box on the floor behind and a little to the right of the guy selling them. He was sitting behind his table, maybe six feet from the box. No fish at the time, as he puts it. When the lights went out, he stood up, took a step or two to the display table, reached across it, and pulled that heavy cloth he uses for a backdrop up over the knives. Then he patted through the cloth to make sure nothing was missing. As he was doing that, he

77

heard the door from the service corridor open."

"Where's that?"

"Right behind the next table. The guy turned around to pick up the box that had these knives in it. Happens it was less than a yard from the door, about which our huckster now feels deep remorse, check? He had to grope around in the dark a bit, and by the time he fell over the chair he'd been sitting on and quit hopping around 'cause he barked his shin, the box wasn't there."

"Uh-oh." Mack, I was sure, was capable of instilling remorse in Caligula.

"Turned up in the service corridor. With eleven knives in it." Mack stopped to look at me, to be sure I could manage the arithmetic. "The one missing is a dagger, silver, seven and a half inches long overall, with a four-inch blade carved with a dragon, tail at the point of the knife. Then there's a three-D head on the dragon and the mouth wide open makes the blade guard, see? and flames or maybe dragon scales carved into the hilt."

I tried to picture the knife. "Fancy."

"Just as dangerous as your average no-nonsense butcher knife. The guy says you could slice a tomato just letting the thing rest on it, no pressure."

Mack wasn't thinking of tomatoes. Neither was I.

"You're looking for somebody who knew the knives were there, and that the door behind the table led to a service corridor," I pointed out.

"Which narrows it down to a couple hundred guys. I asked you a question."

I shook my head. "Can't help. I was talking about UFOs. As a matter of fact, I'd just said something about the lights going out when they went."

"So I heard."

"News travels fast."

"The telephone is a truly marvelous instrument," Mack

remarked, deadpan. "You don't have to show your face or say your name. You don't even have to use your normal voice. The idea, I think maybe, was that you'd set this up. You didn't, of course."

"Thanks, pal."

Mack grinned his cop grin. "Pal, nothing. Physical impossibility. The lights were gone ten minutes, but you kept talking in the dark, so you couldn't have been out of the room for more than a minute, if that. Not long enough to snatch the blade, if you knew it was there. You're not as fast on your feet as you were in high school."

"Thanks. Who was the kind soul who bailed me out with my own big mouth?"

"Yates. One of my three real reliables. Furthermore," said Mack the investigator, "I don't see you getting an accomplice to do the lights. To get that kind of timing, you'd have to use some kind of radio signal. The subpanel for this floor is way the hell the other side of the small meeting rooms, nothing to do with the service corridor that runs past the room you were in."

"Subpanel?"

"Fuse box. Except that it's circuit breakers, of course. All our joker had to do was pull the big one at the top of the panel and run."

"With a flashlight."

"Yeah." Mack's face went blank. "Or a hand on the wall." He sighed. "See you later. Come down to my office in an hour or so. I'll be tied up until then."

He set off down the service corridor, leaving me to square my shoulders and step back through the *Employees Only* door as if I had every right to be there. I gave a good performance, but the only one around to see it was Donovan's ersatz robot, abandoned outside the con suite door.

Inside, Karen, lips parted, was listening to said Donovan

whine about the way editors treat writers. The substance of his complaint seemed to be that he'd been writing for thirteen years and had yet to publish anything.

"Have you tried the fanzines?" somebody in the group asked.

Donovan flushed and muttered something I couldn't hear. I decided the discussion was too technical for me and settled for waving at Karen. She nodded at me. Feeling at loose ends, at least until I could talk to Mack, I decided to go down to the room where we'd dropped my suitcase that morning and call Lydia Eskew. I rode down the elevator accompanied by a superbly patient black Great Dane with little horns stuck on its head and an arrowpoint wagging on the friendly end of its bobbed tail. The master, of course, was dressed to match.

I did restrain myself from stepping on the dragging end of the human devil's tail; I did not restrain a quiet cheer when the elevator doors grabbed it and whipped it off. I like dogs.

Joey was fine. Lydia Eskew was fine. They'd spent a fine morning at the Linden Hills Park, where Joey had had a wonderful time climbing in the spaceship jungle gym. She called out to him, but whatever he was doing was, in six-year-old style, more interesting than saying hello to a Daddy he'd see tomorrow anyway.

"He'll wish he'd come to the phone when he has to go to bed," Mrs. Eskew predicted.

"No, he won't," I said. "He knows a good thing when he sees it. I wouldn't let him stay up as late as you will. But if you know what's good for you, you'd better make sure you've got him stowed away before Karen gets home."

She laughed. We chatted two minutes longer and hung up. A ghost of a thought flitted through my dense skull: something about a radio signal, trying to connect with something I had seen someone do. A button pushed? Eyes closed, I could almost see it. I was already stretched out on the bed. Still getting up the energy to haul myself to my feet, I fell asleep.

The phone woke me. A soft but businesslike female voice identified itself as belonging to Michelle and told me Mack was looking for me.

"Right," I sighed.

Catching sight of myself in the mirror over the dresser, I ran my fingers through what's left of my hair, tucked in the side of my shirt that had come out as I slept, and pronounced myself fit to be seen—not that anyone would notice any irregularity of dress short of stark nakedness in this place. If I could believe Ferraro, maybe not even that.

Mack was studying a floor plan of the hotel when I got down to the security office. He looked up and motioned me to a seat across from him. At the end of the table the old woman with the cat was reading the much-thumbed *Omni*, the cat curled up asleep on the table beside her.

"People's exhibit number one," Mack said, shoving the floor plan across the table. "You are here."

I traced out the plan from the point Mack's thick index finger landed on. Some parts were shaded in. These seemed to be the nonpublic areas. Behind the meeting rooms that opened off the central area was a corridor that ran the width of the wing. Stairs at one end probably were the same ones I'd gone down last night. A second corridor ran perpendicular to the first, served by an elevator next to the public ones but opening in the other direction. There was a second staircase in a wide stairwell beyond the elevator. The electrical subpanel had been marked in red on the landing. Doors from this shorter corridor opened into both the core and the east wing of the hotel, which seemed otherwise separate, no doubt to the relief of the engineers had they but known.

"Here," Mack said, plunking his finger down again, "and here."

One of the spots Mack was interested in, I figured out finally, was the door that led from the huckster room—actually three rooms thrown together by pulling back movable walls—into the service corridor where the box of knives had been found. The other was a door from conference room D, where I'd been lecturing, into the same service corridor. I shoved the map back, pointing to the other two doors into the huckster room.

"I know. That one"—Mack's finger came down on the one farther away from the knives—"was pretty well blocked. Seems the guy there thought having a door right behind his table wasn't such a good idea, so he put a bookcase across it. It would give the fire marshal the pip, but it was there."

"The other one?"

"Hard to get to without falling over two or three pairs of legs."

"So you want to know if somebody left my fascinating lecture to go shopping for knives. Hell, Mack, twenty or twenty-five people must have left while the lights were out. I couldn't tell you which way they went."

"I thought you were going to observe for me."

"Have a heart. It was pitch black in there."

"Yeah. Well." Mack tilted his chair onto its back legs and sighed. "It was a thought."

"Wait," I said. "I did feel a draft."

The chair legs came down. "That's more like it."

"Look, it could have been the ventilation system. I know I heard the fans going a little later."

"Can you give me a time? How long after the lights went out?"

"Let me think." Looking at my watch, I ran over the sequence in my mind: dark, surprise, my own words of exasperation. Another ten or twelve seconds while people began to move and talk. The chair going down, then the draft. "Not for at least fifteen seconds," I estimated. "So, if anybody went through the door in my room—and I don't remember hearing a door open—it wasn't right off the mark."

"Opportunist," said the old woman at the end of the table. Mack glanced at her as if the furniture had spoken. "Knew where the knives were, and how to get there. Took a few seconds to put it all together, and acted on the chance."

"Some chance," Mack said. "He had to know those lights were going to be out long enough to cover him."

The woman licked a finger and turned a page. "Did he?"

"You're saying look for somebody smart and reckless. Is that it?" Mack asked.

The woman shrugged. The cat looked up, yawned, and found a more comfortable arrangement of paws and nose. Mack stared at them a few seconds. No more suggestions were forthcoming.

"Well, I got to think about this some more. Stay cool, J.J.," Mack instructed. "And keep your eyes open, check?"

"Check."

Again at loose ends, I decided to go up to the con suite to see if I could find my wife. The first elevator car that stopped I rejected: the two passengers were my old pal the blond, back in the nearly transparent green dress, and one of the college boys. She seemed to have developed a fair amount of trust in him. When no one stepped through the open doors she broke off the kiss and glanced out with a look of grim triumph. She'd left the dragon behind, I noticed. Not that it was necessary.

The second car that stopped contained a redheaded Amazon almost as tall as Mack and an eight-foot boa constrictor, either of whom looked far less dangerous than the blond. I got in and was invited to pet the snake.

It, at least, was staying cool.

Karen looked politely bored. She greeted me with a small smile that nevertheless must have cracked her cheeks.

"Get some coffee and come talk to me," she said, after introducing me around the circle of writers, who were now apparently telling horror stories about what happens if you *do* get published.

I got us each a big cup of burned coffee from the urn and let Karen lead the way into the third room of the suite, where two women in the near corner were engaged in a tense conversation. Karen jerked her head toward the table farthest from them, and I sat down with raised eyebrows. Apparently she really meant talk and not eavesdrop.

"I hear we missed a few fireworks," she said in a low voice. She reached absentmindedly into a bucket of popcorn and tossed a couple of kernels into her mouth.

"More fireworks?" I glanced at the spot on the floor where the metal tray had been.

She shook her head, chewing. "Not that. Human kind."

"Oh," I said, losing interest.

"Couple of concom members had a loud argument outside the committee office. Apparently veddy bad form, as the British say. One of them accused the other of sabotaging the con. Eyebrows have been raised, literally and verbally. Especially verbally."

"When was this?"

"Oh, sometime before lunch."

"Let me guess. Dan Bascombe and Cass Grenzman."

Karen offered me the popcorn and didn't seem to notice when I blinked. The con was having peculiar effects on her. "Half right. Cass Grenzman accused somebody described as 'what's his name, with the skinny mustache.' "

"Wade Yates," I suggested. Karen shrugged. She didn't know.

"Names were called," she said.

My turn to shrug. "Names are often called in arguments. I've done it myself, though not lately."

"I just thought I'd let you know," she said. "I thought you were spying for Mack and Co."

"If they were arguing outside the con offices that long ago, he knows already," I pointed out. "He's got more serious things to think about."

I told her about the knife.

"From *your* room?" she protested. "Joe, how?"

"Easy. Think about it. He wouldn't have any trouble finding the door with that exit light over it. All he has to do is avoid falling over a chair. The light's too dim for anyone to see by, and up too high to silhouette anybody moving. The service doors aren't locked—they lead to the stairs, and the emergency exits, so they can't be—and the huckster room door is only ten feet away."

"He?"

I stared at her.

"Don't you mean he or she?"

"I guess I do," I said slowly.

"*I'd* choose a pretty knife, if I were going to steal one," she added. "No matter what I planned to use it for."

I thought that over, chewing my lower lip.

"I think Mack had better hope it was a he," Karen continued, "because a man would be more likely to steal something efficient-looking if he planned to use it, don't you think? Like one of those Gurkha things that looks like a flamingo beak. Pretty knives are only for collecting. Joe, would you mind getting me some more coffee?"

On my way through the room with the bar, I got grabbed by the arm. "Hey, man," said Cass Grenzman. "How ya doing?"

"Okay," I said cautiously.

Grenzman glanced at a companion. I half-held my breath. "How'd you like a new experience?" he asked.

"I don't do dope," I said, pulling away.

"Better than dope."

"Ever heard of Killer?" his friend asked.

"I've heard of it."

"Want to play?"

"No, thanks," I said.

The friend grinned at Grenzman. Any minute, the guy was going to start bleeding out his eyeballs.

"Listen, don't turn it down so fast," he said. "Man, this game's got everything. People get excited, you know?"

"Really gets the adrenaline pumping," Grenzman translated.

"Oh, wow. Tell me about it," the friend said. "When you off a guy you really get a rush. Good as coke. First time, man, I had a hard-on."

"No, thanks," I repeated, backing away toward the coffee.

"Told you he was nothing to worry about," Grenzman said to his friend.

Nothing to worry about? I worried vaguely myself, drawing coffee into our cups and putting a spoonful of whitener into my own. I wasn't about to ask Grenzman for an explanation and get nothing but laughed at for my trouble.

When I got back with the coffee, Karen was standing at the window looking out at the view—one of the less prepossessing vistas of our fair city, lacking as it did any buildings of architectural distinction other than the Metrodome with its air-puffed roof.

"Wouldn't you like to jump on that?" she asked, nodding at the tan pillowy shape. "It looks like a giant moonwalk."

She turned away from the window and sat down again, this time closer to the table where the other two women were still talking, and reached for the coffee. Sipping it, she was silent—listening.

I caught the name *Maureen* and listened myself, hoping to identify the faint bell it rang, but could make out nothing else. Apparently, neither could Karen. A few minutes later she glanced at her watch, drank the last of the coffee and, pointing out that she had almost two hours free before the writing workshop she wanted to sit in on, reminded me that we had an empty hotel room five floors below.

"Everybody else is doing it," she said. "Why not us?"

Why not, indeed?

Chapter Eight

WE BLEW THE fifty bucks I'd been paid for the afternoon's talk on a long, lazy dinner. Karen was just as wide-eyed as she'd been at lunch. The fantasy-writing workshop had turned out to be more than she'd bargained for, although for reasons not altogether to do with writing.

"More dragons and fair ladies than you'd ever believe could be so dull," she exclaimed, with a quick smile for the waiter as the scallop appetizer was set in front of her. "But the best part was the other writers. My God, what a bunch of nuts!"

She sampled the scallops and screwed up her eyes in pleasure.

"I should be fair," she amended a moment later.

"Lady Kay, you're fair enough for me, even without a dragon," I said.

I got a don't-be-silly-we're-grown-ups-now look. "No, I mean, I should be kind. Only half of them are nuts. Donovan, of course—no wonder he doesn't get published—and a girl who went on and on about blue unicorns."

"I thought unicorns were white."

"You have no imagination. Hers were blue, with red horns." Karen took a thoughtful sip of wine. "You know, you could just about tell what kind of stuff you were going to hear by how they treated their manuscripts. One guy—I think he must be professional—just had his in a folder with a rubber binder around it. The worst was a kid with ten or twelve stories, each wrapped up with cardboard front and back and, get this, each one in a separate padded envelope so the corners wouldn't get dinged."

"Can't type," I said. "Has to pay for it."

"Not worth the money, believe me. I never heard such tripe in my life."

Her *poulet sauté chasseur* arrived just then. She speared a plump mushroom with her fork, and we settled down to the business at hand.

We got back to the con just in time for the costume contest. The weird outfits that had become familiar over the past twenty-four hours were only half of it. More uncomfortable or more delicate fantasies that had been packed away for the past day and a half appeared, in fabrics ranging from polyester leopard skin to a fine, pale, floating silver stuff Karen called tulle. I saw a single Jedi warrior in a coarse brown robe, although Dr. Who's multicolored scarf dangled from a couple of dozen necks. A few minutes after we arrived, Diz Donovan trundled his robot out of the elevator with an almost cheerful expression on his lean, pale face.

Spotted around the room were Mack's volunteer security crew, among them the twins in costume. Most of them looked pretty nervous, probably because they'd been told about the stolen knife. The fraternity boys weren't much in evidence. They'd either gotten bored and gone home or settled in upstairs with the bheer and or/a friendly fan. The few watching the contest contributed only hoots and whistles to the proceedings.

The parade was about to get underway when the Amazon I'd met on the elevator called for attention. In brass bra and diaphanous trousers, she got it.

"Please," she said. "Don't whistle at me. Not now. It's Kundala." Her voice broke. She cleared her throat and shook that red hair out of her face. Tears glittered in her eyes. "My snake. She's gone."

Into the silence Bascombe said the words we'd all thought. "Escaped, you mean?"

"No, no," she said quickly. "No. Not escaped. Taken."

The silence, if possible, deepened. "Somebody took Kundala?" asked a disbelieving voice from the crowd.

"Yes. And her box. It's so big." She sketched a two-foot-by-three-by-eighteen-inch shape with her hands. "Please, I want her back. She's a pet. If anybody saw someone with her or her box?" She looked hopefully at the faces in the room, but all were blank. "It's no joke. It's not funny."

No one could think of anything to say.

"Well." The woman shrugged. "If anybody sees her, please, *please* let me know? And I'll come get her. And, uh, if somebody wants to return her, you know, unseen? I'll leave my room open until midnight. No, one o'clock. Room six-oh-three. No trouble, I promise, as long as she's okay. I—I guess we'd better get on with the contest."

She stepped back with another toss of her flaming hair, and a smile that didn't quite make it. Bascombe, still the only man in the north wing wearing a white shirt, came forward.

"I know everyone will want to help," he said. "But I just want to say a special word to the volunteers. You gophers see just about every corner of the con, so keep an eye out, please? And you security people, with the headsets, if you even suspect you see the snake, call in."

"Don't forget, even a big snake can crawl into a pretty small space," said a voice from the crowd. The Jedi warrior held his arms aloft for attention. His hood dropped back; I was surprised to see that the warrior was Yates. "Remember that one that got stuck in the trunk of a squad car last summer? They had to pull the car apart to get it out? It was on television. . . ."

The Amazon put her hands over her face.

"So be really, really alert," Yates cautioned.

"How awful," Karen murmured as a rather subdued contest began. "Why would anybody do such a thing?"

I tried to think of as many pranks as I could to be played with an eight-foot boa constrictor and only slowly brought my attention to the contest.

A number of categories had been set up for prizes. The winners were ingenious indeed, but the prize Karen and I liked best was given to April Thorney, who wasn't even wearing her abused jeweled satin. She got a beautifully lettered scroll entitled *Award of Special Merit*, presented with flourishes to match the lettering and a Distinguished Service Medal sculpted out of a disposable aluminum pie tin. She laughed, and she cried, and a lot of the audience did both with her.

Despite that touching episode, there was one further sour note. Diz Donovan won a third prize and thought it should have been a first. The robot got kicked viciously in the side by its maker and scooted across the floor sending people scattering out of its way—only a prelude to a red-faced, heel-drumming temper tantrum the likes of which I hadn't seen since Joey was two and a half. Bascombe got Donovan calmed down and out of the way with creditable speed, and the party adjourned to the tenth floor for bheer.

"I think I just want to go home," Karen said, stepping out of the flow of the crowd toward the elevators. "I've had enough of this."

"I don't blame you," I said. "I wish I hadn't promised Mack I'd stay."

We took the escalator to the first floor, found our way downstairs and through the windowed airlock designed to keep the hotel weather separated from whatever heat or cold the street might toss into the parking garage, and reclaimed the station wagon.

"Give me a call in the morning, okay?" Karen asked,

looking up at me from the driver's seat with an anxious frown. "I . . . Joe, I wish you weren't staying, too."

"Can't run out on Mack now," I said.

"No, of course not. Still, be careful, will you?"

"Sure." I leaned down and kissed the end of her nose. "Roll up that window while you're driving through town, okay?"

"Oh. Yeah."

She rolled it up before starting the car, and I watched the taillights past the top of the ramp before hurrying back through the spooky, half-lit rows of cars into the hotel. I saw no snakes on the way, but then, I didn't stop to examine any shadows.

The first floor of the Wellesford Regal was eerily empty with fans in the con suite and engineers out on the town. I emerged from the stairwell near the elevators and crossed the lobby past the registration desk to the escalators. Beyond the breakfast room someone in the gold-and-blue uniform of a hotel minion was just removing a sign that announced that the pool was closed for maintenance from nine-thirty to ten-thirty. The salad bar restaurant was closed, dimly lit beyond its half-wall of palm trees, chairs upended on the tables. I continued past the mirrored colonnade to the escalators and ascended. Donovan's robot languished in the center of the open reception area, a cylindrical waif with spotlight eyes awry.

The party might have been in the con suite, but as I'd expected Mack was in the con office, alone.

"Karen gone?" he asked, as I poked my head in at the door.

"Just now."

"Tell you the truth, J.J., I'm just as happy."

Happy was one thing Mack didn't look. He carefully lined up the four headsets that weren't in use as I told him about the costume contest. He even managed half a grin over April Thorney's medal and certificate, but it didn't last.

One of the walkie-talkies on the table beside him crackled; he talked into it for a moment or two to someone with a deep voice. "So, take him down to his room," he said after a moment of gabble I couldn't make out. "He isn't? Put him in a cab." He thumbed the transmitter off with a sigh.

"One of my old ladies," he said. "The headsets were a cruddy idea. These cheap things don't have enough power to carry in a steel-frame building, so half the time you can't make out what they're saying, and now nobody but me bothers to think beyond step one, punch the button."

Punch the button. Oh, and call Mack instead of taking a shot at the problem. But wasn't there another button?

Mack cupped his head in his hands and shook it. "Missing boa constrictors, for God's sake. This job was supposed to be my big break. It broke, all right."

A pot of coffee entered the office, borne by a Vulcan twin in full regalia. Mack barely glanced at the girl, though he did remember to smile.

"Thanks, Marie," he said. "The stuff of life."

"I can get you some junk food, if you want."

"Later, maybe. Right now, just this is great."

"It'll prop up your lids. Michelle made it herself." One of Marie's pointed ears leaned suddenly to half-mast. She fiddled with it a moment and got it to stand up straight. "These things hurt, you know?" she said. The ear fell off. "Oh, crap. There's reasons people don't win costume contests."

She exited, reapplying the ear. "Ah," Mack said, of the coffee. "You could stand a spoon up in this. Good stuff."

I poured myself a cup. Any spoon standing in stuff like that would promptly dissolve. "Made any progress toward finding your joker?" I asked.

Mack took a breath and blew it upward, fluttering his mustache. "Guy wears gloves," he said. "And he's careful to smear what he touches. No prints on the fake bombs, no prints on that doorknob, no prints but the owner's on the box of knives, no prints on the light switches, no prints on the wall. Ten will get you twenty there's no prints on that snake when it turns up, either."

"He can't wear gloves all the time," I said.

"Can't he?" Mack gave me a quizzical glance. "Have some more coffee and get your lids propped, J.J. Nine out of ten of those costumes include gloves. And there must be over a hundred of them. Not counting the belly dancers."

"It is a guy?"

"Voice on the telephone to the Health Department was male, and the one that made the bomb threat was male. This still strikes me as a one-man job, though I guess it could be a couple working together—that would explain the knife."

"It hasn't turned up?"

"Have you heard me shouting the jubilee?"

"The knife bothers me," I said. For a moment, I was bothered by something else, something I couldn't quite remember. "It doesn't fit with the rest. The bomb scare was a nuisance, but it didn't hurt anybody, and the firecrackers were even funny. The lights going out didn't hurt—"

Mack shook his head. "You're forgetting the refrigerators, and the tablecloths in the ovens. That could have been real trouble."

"I guess," I agreed, frowning.

"Besides," Mack said, "there's other things to worry about. Like, what happens when one of the Wellesford Regal's nice new cops busts one of these kids for possession? It's only a matter of time. Like I said before, they're not exactly sneaky about what they're smoking. I thought sure we'd lose a few when the on-duty guys came around to take the report on that knife."

"How come you don't ?"

"Bust one?" Mack smiled tightly. "You sound like Yates. I am no longer an officer of the law, check? So I am not about to sweat the small stuff, not on this job. I was warned it would happen, and I made up my mind about that four months ago. Sure, if I had evidence somebody was dealing in big numbers, I'd pass the info along to one of the rent-a-cops and let him handle it. Except one of them's a she, I keep forgetting. But myself? No way. By the time they got done with this crowd, it'd be white helmets and nightsticks all down the line. I got enough trouble."

"I guess."

"Most of them don't get as smashed as I used to on good old Grain Belt," Mack commented.

Rationalizing. The Forrester household budget must be even tighter than I'd thought. For a moment, Mack sat unmoving. Then he shook his head.

"Crap, a missing eight-foot snake! Just what I needed, another crazy thing to worry about."

"Mack, that reminds me. This afternoon Cass Grenzman did something funny. He and a pal of his invited me to play Killer."

"You take him up on it?"

"No, of course not," I said, annoyed. "And then Grenzman turned to the other guy and said, 'I told you he was nothing to worry about.'"

"Mmm," Mack said, with an abrupt nod.

"He said it would be a new experience, meaning the game, I guess. At first I thought he was talking about dope—the other guy had been smoking pot. I'm not sure about Grenzman."

"Like I say," Mack said. "They're not shy." He glanced at his watch. "Almost midnight. Time for the Klingons to come out of the woodwork. I'd better get on the move. Want to come?"

"Where?"

The tight smile flashed again. "Foot patrol. Good experience for rookies."

"Sure," I said, downing the last of my coffee.

As I followed Mack down the hall, I found myself thinking of him as a shield: the cop walk was back. He's a full head taller than I am, though I'm only a couple of inches short of six feet myself. The extra seventy pounds he carries is only about five percent beer gut and getting less so all the time.

"Time for the fun and games," Mack said, shoving through a door labeled *Employees Only*. "Bascombe and the twins are monitoring the skinny-dipping to keep the fraternity boys behaving like their mothers think they do."

"What are *we* doing?"

"Taking sensor readings of this quadrant of the galaxy."

"Come again?"

"Keeping the peace."

We encountered one of the rent-a-cops at the top of the first set of stairs we climbed. "What's going down?" Mack asked.

"They're playing," the cop said, with a disgusted grimace. "Laser Tag in the parking ramp. In here we got World War II going on, plus the spacemen."

"How about the weapons?"

"Every one I've seen that needs it has the tape and the Ping-Pong ball," the man reported. "They're good about that."

Mack nodded. "We'll be patrolling, too," he said. "You heard about the snake?"

"Snake?"

"Eight-foot boa constrictor missing with cage, but I'll buy

you a drink if the thing's still in it. You on our frequency?"

Glancing at the radio clipped to his belt, the officer nodded. "You don't transmit too good," he said. "If you sent anything out about the snake, I missed it."

"Cheapo headsets. Can't be helped." The sound of gunfire down the corridor brought all our heads up. "Caps," Mack diagnosed.

"Right," the other cop agreed.

"Keep your eyes open. The jerk with the snake is likely to use it somehow. See you."

"Mack, I just remembered something," I said, as the rent-a-cop headed down. "Did Bascombe tell you about the videotapes?"

"Yeah, he told me about the videotapes," he said in a tired singsong.

"You haven't heard anything from the vice squad, have you?"

"Of course not."

"Then that must be still to come."

Mack shook his head. "Nope. Bascombe told me, he told all the badgers, he told the concom, he told half the gophers. For all I know, he called the vice squad and told *them*."

"Defused," I said.

"Defused. No more trick, no more trap."

I began to have some insight into foot patrol. Twice, we met one of the Killer players. Once, we were shot at by a guy in camouflage. Mack, who had involuntarily flattened himself against the wall as the gun came around a corner, shook his finger at the player and walked on. A whispered apology floated after us.

"He ought to be glad you don't have your gun," I said.

"Nah." Mack grinned and shook his head. "That doesn't even sound like a gunshot."

"It did to me."

"Not sharp enough, not loud enough. And the purple ball showed up real good." He glanced up at the unprotected fluorescent lamps that marched down the center of the ceiling. "This kind of light helps."

"What happens when one of the rent-a-cops gets shot at?"

"Nothing. I clued them in."

My insight into foot patrol began to include boredom. I yawned till my ears cracked, despite Michelle's coffee.

"Quit that," Mack protested.

We slogged on, down a set of stairs that looked identical to the one I'd used when the hotel was evacuated, yawning in tandem.

Shifting to public corridors, we ran into Yates. "You on tonight?" Mack asked.

"Sure."

"Good. When?"

Yates, still a Jedi warrior, pulled up his sleeve and glanced at his watch. "Half an hour. You need me now?"

"Half an hour will do," Mack said. "But I'll be glad of you then. The Klingons are playing, and Grenzman's gang just started."

"At least that will keep him out of the pool," Yates remarked, sounding not at all interested.

"But it won't keep him or his pals out of the engineers' hair. I need some self-starters on duty. Right now the only ones I've got are Bascombe and the twins, and by now they must be running on empty."

"I promised somebody—" Yates said.

"Take your time." Mack gave him a small, Royal-Family wave, and we headed back into the service stairwell.

We'd made a full round and were starting over by the time Yates reported. He signed on over the headset, and Mack told him to take over from the twins while we continued our patrol. On the fourth floor we met another of the rent-a-cops.

"How's it going?" Mack asked.

"Not too bad," the cop said. "We got the first group thinning out some, but there's another bunch started playing."

"Yeah, I heard. The soldiers."

"That's what they call themselves," the rent-a-cop said scornfully. "Any of them ever saw the front side of a recruiting sergeant, you could have fooled me."

A murmur came up the stairwell as Mack told the cop about the missing snake and they chatted on. A couple of dead Killer players, maybe, or another security patrol. "In the laundry?" said one of the voices from below, suddenly clear, but still eerie after its trip up the well. "You kidding me?"

Three reports sounded from above, but neither Mack nor the cop paid any attention. Caps again, I guessed. "How long does this go on?" the cop asked.

"Till dawn's early light," Mack said.

"All night! Don't they ever wind down?"

"Not so's you'd notice."

"Where'd you find that?" asked the ghost from below. "Who—"

I'd already gone down two steps and parked my butt on the handrail, waiting. Another shot sounded, louder than the others, and then a second. I was still playing it cool when Mack and the rent-a-cop rushed past me.

"Don't move an inch," Mack shouted back at me. "That was the real thing."

Chapter Nine

I DIDN'T MOVE an inch. Not for at least thirty seconds.

Several things happened almost at once. Down below, a door opened but didn't slam. A second off-duty cop rushed past me as the other two sets of pounding footsteps reached the bottom of the stairwell. Three or four voices engaged in a quick, urgent conversation, and two doors opened in quick succession, one fainter than the other.

Then, since the voices sounded urgent but not alarmed, I stood up as quietly as I could and crept down two flights of gritty cement steps. The eight inches of the first floor I could see over the railing showed me nothing, so I moved on down.

"Halt right there," snapped a woman in uniform.

A very large gun covered me.

The woman behind the gun crouched over one of the soldiers in khaki fatigues, who had collapsed just inside the exit door, head tilted back toward me, knees bent. One arm, his right, was bent near his head, the other flopped over his belly. His upper lip was smeared with blood, and a crimson pool, still sluggishly finding its way along the slight downward slope of the floor toward the outside door, surrounded his torso.

"Hold it," Mack said, somewhere still out of sight. "J.J.?"

"Yes," I admitted.

"He's all right."

The gun pointed at the floor and the woman's hand came away from the soldier's throat. "No pulse," she said. "He's gone."

Even foreshortened and bloodied, the face looked familiar. I wished the officer had closed the man's eyes.

"Who?" I asked.

"Cass Grenzman," Mack said.

The woman levered herself to her feet and holstered her gun, and the cop who'd been talking to us when the serious shooting started slipped back through the door from the public corridor.

"Nobody saw anyone go back this way," he said. "There's a guy setting up tables in the breakfast room, and that's where this little chunk of corridor goes to."

I took one more step down, cursing my curiosity at the same time I wanted to satisfy it.

"I thought I told you to park yourself, J.J.," Mack said. "Do yourself a favor and listen once in a while."

I sat down on the middle of the stairs. Nobody said anything else, and nobody looked at the fallen man but me. Grenzman's pants were soaked, not with blood. Urine. It took me a while to figure that out, and then I wished I hadn't.

I'd been right about the stairwell. It was the same one I'd come down during the evacuation the night before. Past the landing where Grenzman had bought it, the stairs went on to the garage under the north wing. Beyond this small, well-lighted space and separated from it by a length of yellow chain hanging from two movable standards was a large, dim area, empty except for several carts of dirty linen and a couple of hand trucks parked against the far wall. Double lift doors, each big enough to admit a large van, but closed, led into the alley. Opposite them was a door marked *Kitchen* and another with the ubiquitous *Employees Only*. The service elevator, down and waiting with its doors open, spilled a streak of yellow light across the floor.

"Was that elevator down, Mack?" asked the cop we'd been talking to. "When we got here, I mean."

Mack studied the stripe of light from the elevator, frowning. "Dunno," he said finally. "Damn, I saw that door open to the alley and that was all I could look at."

"Likewise."

Above me, a latch clicked stealthily. Everyone but me looked up. I tried. My back and neck had turned to stone. I didn't hear another sound until a stricken voice behind me asked, "What's happening?"

"Cass Grenzman got shot," I said.

"Oh, no," a Klingon adolescent said. He stepped heavily down and sank onto the step beside me. The weapon he carried would never have been mistaken for anything of this world, even without a purple Ping-Pong ball. "Is he gonna be all right?"

"No," Mack said.

The boy looked at his phaser, a silvery hunk of plastic. With a puzzled frown he set it on the step beside him. The silence grew. The boy breathed in and opened his mouth, but whatever the question was, it died on his tongue. Outdoors I heard a metallic clang. Dumpster lid? I wondered.

"Where'd you come from?" Mack asked the kid. "What floor?"

"Third."

"You didn't see anybody running by," Mack stated. The boy shook his head. Anyone passing him would have had to pass Mack and two uniformed cops first.

After what seemed like half an hour, but was probably under five minutes, a siren sounded down the block, and the three standing near the body looked up in relief.

The other two rent-a-cops came in from the street, breathing hard. "Nowhere," one of them reported. "That's a long, clear alley, pretty clean, nowhere to hide but the dumpsters. The doorman happened to be standing on the corner, looking down the street for a cab. According to him, nobody ran out. He'd have noticed, he says."

"What does that leave?"

"Not a damn thing, far as I can see," said the other searcher. He holstered his gun and circled to stand at the inner door. The door opened.

"Bascombe," Mack said. Two of the officers nodded.

"Oh, my God!" Bascombe exclaimed, staring at the figure on the floor. "Cass! He's not dead!"

"Seems so."

Bascombe took a step forward. Mack put a hand on his chest to stop him. "Don't," he said. "You could mess up the evidence, and you can't do anything for him."

"How do you know? Did you call an ambulance?"

The policewoman jerked her head toward the exit. "That's it coming," she said in a gentle voice. "But don't get your hopes up. I don't think they can help."

The siren wound down as she spoke, and one of the cops stepped over to the outer door to let in a pair of paramedics.

"Doesn't look like much we can do," one of them said after a quick check of the body. "Right through the heart, twice, bet you anything. We'd better leave him for the medical examiner."

While they made their examination, Bascombe had been busy with his headset. The door behind him opened again. Wade Yates walked through, somewhat out of breath. He'd shed his Jedi warrior costume since I'd seen him almost an hour before, and pulled a leather hat low over his eyes.

"What took you so long?" Bascombe demanded.

"Christ, Dan, you said hurry and I ran like hell. I got here as fast as I could," he protested. "Jesus," he added, catching sight of the body as the paramedic got to his feet. "Is that—"

"Cass," Bascombe told him, his voice sticking.

Yates began to circle, as if he wanted a better look at

104

Grenzman's face, and backed off as one of the cops stopped him.

"Poor bastard," he said, rather blankly.

Bascombe's headset crackled. "Let's not start another convention," Mack suggested. "I want you guys to stay available, but let's leave Officer Reid in charge and the rest of us get out before we muck up the evidence."

He collected a nod of agreement from the off-duty cops, and they escorted Bascombe and Yates back through the service door.

"What about them?" called one of the men left behind, jerking his thumb at the boy and me.

Mack looked back through the door at the body sprawled at the bottom of the stairs, and then at me. "They could go up the stairs and meet us. I'm taking everybody to the con office."

Officer Reid squinted at us, her lower lip under her teeth.

"The older guy was with Forrester and me when we heard the shots," said the cop we'd been with.

"I'll vouch for him," Mack said. "He's a friend. J.J., you'll hang onto our pal there and make sure he reports to the con office. Check? Keep him quiet, and keep your own fat mouth shut. The fewer people know about this the better. For the moment," he added, as Bascombe began to protest. "I don't want the whole world trying to jam into this stairwell."

I glanced at the boy, who nodded.

Reid shrugged and looked toward the street door, where the paramedics were conferring. "Where the hell's the damn patrol?" she asked, which I took as permission to leave.

The street door opened as I reached the top of the stairs, and a uniformed cop came through. I paused to watch.

"Morning, Carl," one of the rent-a-cops said. "Look out for that wedge. It was in the door."

The new officer glanced down and let the door close gently against the battered wooden wedge. It suddenly occurred to me that I no longer had an advocate present. I led the Klingon boy around the bend of the stairs and through the service door into the public corridor.

"Was that blood I smelled?" he asked.

"Partly," I said.

"And he, uh, he peed?"

"Happens," I said.

We made a short detour to a men's room to let the kid throw up, so it took a few extra minutes to get to the con office. I found the rent-a-cop perched on the end of the table, swigging Vulcan coffee. Mack had claimed the overstuffed chair, now near the door, and lounged back in it, one ankle propped on the opposite knee, fingers tented. Bascombe and Yates—Yates with his hands clasped on the edge of the table and Bascombe resting his face on his folded arms—sat next to each other at the other end of the table from the cop.

"Well, J.J., you did it again," Mack said.

"Not me," I said. "This one's yours."

"By ten seconds."

The boy was about thirteen, pudgy, as so many of the fans seemed to be, with a thick dark fuzz on the upper lip of a pale baby face. He headed straight for the back wall of the room, slumped against it, and slid down to sit on the floor. I sat more conventionally opposite Yates and absentmindedly tried the coffee pot, but it was empty.

"Some coming," Mack said.

Bascombe snorted. "Should have sent up to the con suite for beer," he said. "Or called room service for a bottle of vodka."

"Upset?" asked Mack.

106

"Hell, yes, wouldn't you be? I can't pretend Cass was a close friend, but I've known him five years. We worked together on this con for months. And now . . . hell, and at a con! Yeah, it shakes me up."

Mack nodded slightly, his fingers still matched. Any minutes he'd start chewing his mustache.

"Let's not discuss the case," said the uniformed cop.

I heard a distorted voice from behind me and turned. One of the twins sat cross-legged on the floor, listening to a headset and taking notes. The voice had escaped when she eased the earphone and smoothed back her hair. She gave me a wan smile and wrote something on the pad on her knee.

"What's that?" I asked Mack.

"Keeping tabs on the rest of the game. They don't know yet."

Bascombe bit his lips and looked off to one corner of the ceiling. "Christ, what do we do now?" he asked of the Wellesford Regal's cobwebs.

"We sit," Yates said. His hands had started shaking. He let them drop into his lap and stared at them.

Sue Evers, the redheaded committee member who had come into my lecture room after the blackout that afternoon, tapped at the doorframe. Even in jeans and a faded T-shirt she looked elegant. "What?" she asked.

"Cass Grenzman," Bascombe said. He cleared his throat and, as Mack had done, carefully aligned the pair of headsets on the table in front of him. "He's dead."

"Dead!"

"Playing Killer," Bascombe said. "Somebody shot him for real."

"Oh," Sue breathed.

Her mouth stayed open, but she didn't find anything else to say. She came slowly to the table, grabbed the back of the chair next to me with both hands, and leaned on it.

"We called everybody," Bascombe said. "Most of them should be here soon."

"Maureen?"

Bascombe shook his head.

"She taking it hard?"

"Couldn't find her."

Suddenly it connected. My friend the blond was the Maureen in question. Cass Grenzman's girl, slung prettily on his arm just last night. She'd had no badge on that gauzy dress then, but Bascombe had called her by name. Well, well, well. The slender redhead was running through a list of suggestions for Bascombe, to each of which he nodded yes. He'd had somebody look there, and no Maureen. I thought a general bed check might locate the woman, but I kept my mouth shut. They'd all been jolted out of their fantasy world pretty rudely. Anything I had to say would go right on by.

I heard a muffled sob from the back of the room and went to hunker next to the Klingon boy, for whatever comfort it was worth.

Chapter Ten

OTHER MEMBERS OF the concom straggled in over the next half hour. The media were a lot faster. Bascombe managed to fend off a gaggle of reporters by promising a statement the next morning. After several minutes of argument, the TV lights had been turned off and even Channel 7 had flapped away home. Sue Evers had taken charge of the Klingon, who was eventually paroled to his older sister and hustled off to bed.

For a couple of minutes after the reporters left, Bascombe speculated aloud about the open outside door to the service area. Yates chimed in with the idea that some mundane coming through that open door with intention of mugging someone might have panicked at the sight of a guy in camouflage carrying a hand gun, shot him, and run. The cop, somebody Mack seemed to know named Al, pointed out that the blind alley had been searched within two minutes and that people on the street outside the hotel had seen no one run from it.

Mack gazed at him, head tilted, and Al added that they really shouldn't talk about the case until the investigating team arrived. After that, beyond giving the bare bad news as others arrived, no one seemed able to talk.

The telephone rang, and Bascombe picked it up. "Yes, he's here," he said, looking at Mack, who took the receiver from him and grunted into it a few times.

He hung up, jerked his head at me, and said to Al, "We're going downstairs to answer a few questions. You should have three more coming, check?" He strode out of the room, officer of the law on urgent business again, with me tagging after him wondering what was up.

"Anybody else, I'd have left him behind," he told me. "But I know about you and dead-ohs. Especially if there's a UFO anywhere near the neighborhood."

"Stuff it," I said.

"Hell, now all you have to do is *talk* about the suckers."

"Mack—"

"How is it, J.J.," he continued, sounding aggrieved, "that every time you and I and a UFO come together, some poor jerk gets snuffed?"

"Not my idea," I said. I almost had to jog to keep up, a factor that did nothing to improve my temper.

"Do yourself a favor and keep your mouth shut."

"You could do with a dose of your own advice."

"Might as well talk to a Mack with the surname of Truck. When we get downstairs the only thing I want open is your eyes and ears. You hear me? Let them ask the questions."

That piece of advice suited me fine. We hurried down the escalator and past the breakfast room toward the stairwell. As we went I remembered to make allowances for sleeplessness and strain. And I remembered something else.

"Mack, Karen told me something this afternoon that somebody ought to know. Cass Grenzman had a loud argument with someone earlier today and accused him of sabotaging the con. No name, but the description matches Yates."

"Yates!" Mack shook his head and snorted. "Nah, that was Diz Donovan."

"Donovan? You're sure? The person Karen talked to said something about a long mustache."

"Try *unt immed*."

"I can't see Donovan putting together all these tricks," I

110

protested. "He doesn't seem, well, quite all there."

"He's there," Mack said. "Royal pain in the ass, but he's every bit there. So was I. During the argument, I mean."

We reached the first floor service door. Mack snatched it open. The glare in the stairwell half-blinded me. The photographer had arrived and set up some lights for taking pictures. A heavy-browed man in a brown knit shirt and jeans detached himself from the group near Cass Grenzman and came toward us.

"Hi, Mack," he said, hand out to shake. "And, uh, Jamison, isn't it? How's your family?"

"Fine." I put on a grin to go with it: this guy, whose name I couldn't for the life of me remember, had worked on the case when Karen and Joey had been kidnapped, almost five years ago now. I got my hand gripped, too, but the detective had already turned his attention back to Mack.

"You found the body?"

Mack nodded. "With one of your off-duty officers. Kimski, his name is."

"What's Jamison doing here?"

"He was with us when we heard the shots. There were two."

The expressionless eyes under the heavy brows flicked over me. I'd just acquired a small value. "Was the face clean when you found it?"

Mack shook his head. "Smear of blood on the upper lip."

"How long was that after you heard the shooting?"

"Long enough to go down three floors two steps at a time. Ten seconds?"

"We'll time it, if we have to. You're sure about that smear?"

"Absolutely. What's up?"

"Blood on his right hand and upper lip, but no injury to either. Looks at first sight as if he dipped the hand in his own blood and smeared it across his mouth as he was dying."

"Shot twice? In the heart, the paramedic said."

"He'd have had a few seconds, the M.E. tells me. Maybe five or ten."

Mack stared toward the body, chewing on his mustache. "Weird," he pronounced.

"Kimski tells me you're directing security for a convention that's going on here, and this guy was on some kind of committee running it."

Mack nodded. "Check. They call this committee the concom. There's fifteen on it, counting this guy, and they should all be somewhere in the hotel. Can't locate a couple of them, but the others I told to report to the committee office on the second floor. I left a rent-a-cop with them, one of your guys, and the chairman's on the phone trying to get hold of the others."

"Disagreements there?"

"If the Naval Observatory gave them the time, these guys would give them an argument. Nothing that made me expect this, though. It's like it's a game with them."

"Kimski says the street door was open."

"Check. Had one of those wooden wedges between it and the jamb, held it open maybe an inch and a half. Two of your guys doing some off-duty checked the alley. Didn't find anybody."

"You?"

Mack clapped his hands to his jeans-covered hips. "Unarmed. I kept an eye on the scene while Kimski checked the first floor hall and called in. Officer Reid showed up a few seconds after we did, and she looked the service area over. Nobody."

From this angle, I could see Grenzman's cap pistol, half under his left side. The Ping-Pong ball had torn loose and rolled an inch or so, until the clear tape that had held it to the gun stopped it, and the green tape around the muzzle of the gun almost glowed in the fluorescent light. The smear of blood across Grenzman's face looked grotesque, a drying brownish line that trailed down beside his mouth on the right side. I thought his left hand might be clutched around something, but couldn't tell for sure. Someone had pulled plastic bags over his hands and taped them around his wrists.

"What's the deal here?" the detective asked. "They playing cowboys and injuns or what?"

Where's Cass's headset? I wondered.

"Close." Mack explained the game and the meaning of the tape and the purple ball. The detective scratched his jaw and nodded. "You oughta collect the rest of the players," Mack suggested. "They might be able to do a little reconstruction for you."

"We've intercepted a few. Got any idea what this thing is?" the detective asked, pointing to the laser gun the Klingon boy had left behind on the step.

"That arrived afterwards."

The detective narrowed his eyes, nodding after each phrase as Mack described how the laser gun got there. He asked Mack a few more questions, me none, and told us to keep ourselves available. Mack warned him about the missing snake, assured him he could find us in the concom office, explained where the office was, and we left.

"Does available mean awake?" I asked.

"I sure as hell hope not." Mack yawned. "I get the chair," Mack said.

We walked back into the middle of a sniping session and got caught in the crossfire.

"You know damn well it was one of you," Wade Yates was shouting as Mack opened the door. "Who the hell else? Every damn one of those weapons was checked personally by one of us, and they were all fakes, every one of them. Who had real guns? Only the cops."

"How the fuck do you know you checked every weapon?" the cop, still Al, demanded.

"Hooo, hooo," Mack said, patting the air down in front of him with both hands as he advanced cautiously into the room.

"Wade," Bascombe warned.

"I told you we should have outlawed Killer," Donovan was saying. "I told you. You didn't listen to me. You never listen to me," and more in the same line, very distinctly in a loud, high, whining monotone that reminded me of fingernails scraping a blackboard.

"Goddamn jerk-off game," the cop said through his teeth. "You were asking for it!"

"Sure it's a jerk-off game," Yates yelled. "I wouldn't play it in a million years. And one damn good reason is because I'm scared I'll get offed by some fascist rent-a-cop."

"Wade!" Bascombe shouted, grabbing Yates's shirt to try to keep him in his seat.

"You should have listened," Donovan droned.

"Hooo," said Mack. "Hooo."

"You want to spend the night locked up, buddy?" the cop asked Yates. "We got a real convenient jail a couple of blocks from here."

"Hooo—"

"Now somebody's dead—"

"—personally will drag you by the ears—"

"Itchy trigger-fingers—"

"SHUT UP!"

Everyone stopped midword but Donovan, who said, "Any responsible con would have outlawed—"

"Later, Diz," Bascombe said.

Donovan's mouth kept moving, but his voice stopped coming out.

114

"Now that I have what passes for your attention," Mack said, "may I point out that this is no time for recrimination. We are all very tired, and some of us aren't thinking our clearest. Let me remind you that the investigation is only just beginning. All possibilities, I repeat, *all* possibilities will be considered by the investigating officers." He took a deep breath. "Including that of a mistake on the part of one of the off-duty officers hired by the hotel. Which, I might add, I consider unlikely. This is not the first unusual incident to affect this con. Remember?"

Donovan shot Mack an alarmed glance and shut his mouth with a snap. Yates sat back, tugging at his mustache, and Bascombe let out a long, slow breath through tightened lips. Al nodded.

"I would not be surprised in the least if the officers in charge talk to every single person in this hotel this weekend. Murder investigations are very thorough, I assure you." Mack stopped and surveyed the faces turned toward him. "Okay, are we all civilized again?"

"Yes," Yates barked, his expression still that of a Celt in the fury of war. At least it was no longer matched by the cop's.

Mack looked around the table and smiled. "I'm starving," he said. "I bet everybody else is, too. Any chance of getting some food down here, Dan?"

"Yeah, sure." Bascombe, blinking, reached for the telephone. "I'll get a gopher to run something down from the con suite."

A ripple of relaxation went around the table at the prospect of eating. The cop's shoulders came out of their hunch. He glanced at Mack, a glance between professionals, and nodded once. Mack shrugged.

Mack finished his tour through the huckster room and chained the last door behind him.

"Those books damn well better be able to take care of themselves," he said. "I'm bushed. And I'm damned if I'll sleep on that mattress." He'd torn loose the springs of the camp cot provided the night before. The mattress was only about an inch and a half thick. I had an extra bed in my room, and that was where we were headed.

The reception area lights had been dimmed. At this hour parties had adjourned to private rooms and more congenial public spaces, and the place was deserted except for Donovan's robot, still standing disconsolately in the center of the floor. We got into the elevator and found a girl in a terrycloth robe whose long, dripping hair had left a dark patch on the worn carpet. She gave us a nervous glance and began to get off, then looked more closely at Mack. "Aren't you the security man?" she asked. "Is it true? Did somebody get killed?"

"Yeah."

"Who? What happened?"

"Cassius Grenzman. He was shot playing Killer."

The girl shuddered and pulled her robe a little tighter. The pink badge pinned to the pocket tilted into the light. "I should have guessed," she said. "That guy was a murder waiting to happen. He hurt people, you know?"

"Like what?"

"Beat up on them and like that. Last summer he gave a friend of mine some bad dope. God, he was sick! And I bet you anything Cass knew all about it. He'd been pissed off at my friend a few days before that. I don't know what kind of world we're living in," she added, shaking her head. "You can't even trust a fan anymore. Can you beat it?"

"Sad, isn't it?" Mack said. "You s'pose he gave bad dope to any other people he was angry with?"

"Who knows?" She tightened her lips and shook her head, exhaling a strong aroma of bheer. "You didn't know Cass. Nobody should get on his bad side, it just makes

116

trouble. Easier to slide by and walk away. I know that's a terrible thing to say—"

"Terrible," Mack agreed hastily. "Say, would you be willing to talk to the police about this? They're set up across the hall from the con office, now."

"The cops?" She hesitated. "Gol, I don't know about cops."

"To catch a murderer?"

"But what if it was a fan?"

The elevator stopped. Mack put his thumb on the *door open* button and held it there. "Even a fan shouldn't get away with murder," he suggested.

"No, I guess not." She was pretty sizzled herself, on that bheer and something else, presumably better stuff than Cass had given her friend. "I guess I'll put some clothes on and go talk to them. But I wouldn't have to say my friend's name, would I? I mean, he's not at the con."

"He might know some other people that got hurt," Mack pointed out.

The girl examined her hands, water-wrinkled and bluish in the elevator's fluorescent light. "I don't think they got all those dangerous chemicals out of the pool when they cleaned it," she said.

"How about it?" Mack insisted.

She hesitated, picking at her fingers. "I better ask him before I say his name."

"You do that." We got off the elevator, and the doors slammed shut behind us as if they'd gotten impatient.

"What was the name on that badge?" Mack asked me.

"Samantha the Sapient," I said.

"That's what I thought, only I didn't want to squint. Bifocals next, J.J.," he added, sighing. "Where's your key?"

I dug the key out of my pocket and opened the room door. Mack flipped on one bedside lamp and fell, fully-dressed, onto the nearest bed.

Not to sleep. He rolled to half-sit, picked up the telephone and dialed. "Bascombe?" he said. "Mack Forrester. You know a girl calls herself Samantha the Sapient? Could you run that through your computer and find out who she is and what room she's in? ... I met her in the elevator, and she said something that made me think she might give us a line on Cass Grenzman's murder—something about sharing out some bad dope last summer ... Yeah, I can see that ... No, I called you first ... You swear to me? ... Yeah, it could wait till morning, I guess. Don't forget they've got your wavelength."

He hung up. By that time I'd stripped to my underwear and claimed the other bed for my own. I hoped Sammy the Wise had enjoyed her swim.

"Old habits die hard," Mack remarked.

"Aren't you calling the detectives?"

"All in good time." He glanced at his watch, frowning.

"What gives?"

Mack cut short a glance at me with a blink, still frowning. "Christ," he said. "This mess. And it looked so *easy*. That's what gets me, J.J."

"This job?" I guessed.

"I could pull it out," he said, not to me but to a pseudo-painting of a ship in full sail that hung on the opposite wall. "I could still pull it out, if I could do the fingering." The frown stayed.

Till morning? Had he meant he'd wait to tell the police about Samantha the Sapient until tomorrow? But what if she decided to go on her own tonight? The friend she wanted to talk to wasn't at the con. *They've got your wavelength*. I stared at him as he silently worked his mouth, still frowning at the ship. Three kids and a wife.

"I wish to hell I knew what Grenzman meant when he said you wouldn't be any trouble."

"Got me. Maybe that I wouldn't interfere with their game?"

"How could you?"

Good question. "Mack, I just remembered something. Where's Grenzman's headset? I didn't see it downstairs."

The glance I got seemed relieved. "You think he had it?"

"Sure, didn't he borrow it to play the game?"

"You know, you're right." Mack sat up against the headboard of the bed, his left thumb pressed into his cheek, index finger stroking his mustache, the better to chew on it. "Could've been under him, I guess."

"All of it? Phones, too?"

Mack folded his arms behind his head. "I knew you had eyes," he said, with a twitch of smile. "Now, why would you want to get the headset away from him?"

"To keep him from calling for help." I bit off the word "obviously" before it got out.

"And *how* would you get it away from him? If he thought he was going to need help?"

"Grab it?"

"He'd have yelled, check? We'd have heard him, we were in the same stairwell. Which means," Mack told the Wellesford Regal's seascape, "that *if* he had it with him and *if* he gave it away, he didn't know he needed help, and most likely he was giving it to somebody he knew."

"Or a cop," I said.

Mack gave me another cut-short glance. "But hell, the guy knew everybody," he said, as if he hadn't heard me. "Even your friend Ferraro of the UFOs. And why would he hand it over?"

"If the person who asked for it had a reason to use it?"

"That cuts things down considerably, doesn't it? Like to about twenty people, the concom and my security team."

"And the rent-a-cops."

Mack sighed. "No cop shot that jerk," he said. "What the hell for? J.J., I'm telling you, all of them knew about that damnfool game, they knew the guns weren't real."

"People make mistakes," I said.

"They knew about the game," Mack said with emphasis. "All it takes is half a second. Even on duty, no games, a cop's gonna hesitate just that one half-second. He's got to have a damn good reason before he blows a guy away. He doesn't want Internal Affairs taking him apart because he was a little too quick on the trigger, check? What if he offed some innocent bystander? And these guys weren't on duty."

"Hold it," I said, thinking back. "Grenzman was talking to somebody." What the hell had I heard? "Something about laundry. Or something being in the laundry. And then he asked about something, like he'd just seen something."

"What?"

"Hell, Mack, I don't know. Could something in the laundry be an excuse for handing over a headset?"

"The snake?"

I shrugged. Maybe. Put the snake in one of those canvas trucks. It shows up to be washed with the Wellesford Regal's sheets and gives somebody the shock of his life. But so what?

A start on an idea, Mack called it. We got no further in the next five minutes. Reminding us both that if anything odd turned up in the laundry the police would be sure to find it and further that he himself was now a civilian, Mack kicked off his shoes, crossed his legs at the ankle, and started to snore.

I turned off the lamp and pulled the Wellesford Regal's lemon yellow sheet over my shoulders. I remember wondering whether Joy Forrester had ironed it as I fell asleep myself.

Chapter Eleven

SUNLIGHT BEATING AT my eyelids woke me up.

Mack was gone. He'd slept on the bed, not in it, leaving a badly wrinkled bedspread as evidence of a restless night and no other sign he'd been there. I sat up and looked at the curtains, pulled a couple of feet open, the source of my discomfort. Or—no—Mack was the source of my discomfort. He'd been up to look out the window sometime in the night, thinking of who knew what.

After a quick shower I decided against concom doughnuts, dropped off my bag in the con office so I could check out whenever I had time, and headed for the Wellesford Regal's breakfast room. I was earlier today than yesterday, and the restaurant was crowded; that is, at least half the tables had at least one person sitting at them. I'd hoped to see Mack, but couldn't spot him or anyone else I knew. I was about to follow the head waiter to a table for one when someone leaned out from a table behind a palm tree and called to me.

"Will you be joining the gentlemen, sir?" the head waiter inquired, his attention already elsewhere.

My "yes" seemed a bit superfluous.

I threaded my way across the room, sat down with three engineers, and felt as if I'd clicked into place.

"Where've you been keeping yourself, J.J.?" asked the guy who'd waved me over. "Haven't seen you in a year. You know Steve and Rich?"

Nods all around. I'd worked with all of them at one time or another. Engineering jobs sometimes resemble musical chairs. My own twelve-year stay with one company, at my age, is a bit unusual.

"I sort of expected to see somebody I knew before this," I said. "But we seem kind of insulated—"

"I'll say. This conference had every other minute scheduled as it was, and besides that they're trying to shoehorn in everything we missed Friday night. This is the first meal we've had on our own."

"That explains it," I said. "How've you been, Chuck?"

"Not bad. I saw your name up on the program board yesterday. Still chasing flying saucers, I see."

"These days I wait for them to come to me," I said, taking the menu that had been shoved in front of my face by yesterday's shuffling waiter. "I'm a project coordinator now. Half the time I'm lucky if I get a minute to say hello to my wife."

"Aren't we all?" Steve said.

"The sci-fi program looks a lot more interesting than the bunk we're hearing," Chuck continued. "I noticed you're part of a panel discussion later this morning. Think you could sneak me in?"

I shrugged. "Maybe I can borrow a badge for you somewhere. You'd have to promise not to object to the name on it, though. Some of them are fairly wild."

"Hey, I'm not blind!" Chuck said, grinning. "I've seen what walks through the lobby. I'll wear antennae, if that helps, or a bearskin."

"You don't have the boobs to hold it up," Rich said.

Chuck grinned. "Who said anything about how big the bearskin had to be?"

"When did you come back from California?" Rich asked.

"Me? Steve's the one in California."

"Joke," Rich informed us gloomily.

"Comes of moving to Massachusetts," Steve said.

"Death to the sense of humor. Why anyone would want to live on Route 128 when the Silicon Valley is lying there—"

"Shaking," said Rich.

"—in all its glory, waiting—"

"And shivering—"

The waiter shuffled back with a carafe, and I turned my cup right side up. The coffee had a fifty-fifty chance of being hot.

"Or if you can't get me in, maybe Diz Donovan can," Chuck said, grimacing at his first sip of coffee. We'd lost; it was tepid.

"You know Diz?" I asked.

"He's a technician in my group," said my former co-worker as the waiter began taking Rich's order. "Weird as they come, but damn good at his job. For him, I'll even spread a napkin on the desk when I open a bag of corn chips." Chuck grinned again. "Keeps the bugs out of the machines."

"I don't get you."

"Haven't you hit that side of Diz? He's a nut on hygiene. I think he really believes that if you leave one little crumb around someplace it's gonna mean cockroaches chomping on the silicon. Maybe on the software, too, for all I know."

"Sounds hard to work with."

Chuck laughed. "Yeah, you could say that. Worth it, though. He can make any machine on earth stand up and dance to your tune. My boss calls him the Sorcerer."

"I worked with him at CDC before we both left," Steve put in. "Never saw anything like it. Too bad he didn't get his degree. He'd have been one hell of an engineer."

"Well, we all know why he didn't, don't we," Chuck commented, and turned to the waiter to order the Sunday Breakfast Special.

"Why?" I asked Steve, as the waiter scribbled.

"Thinnest skin known to man," Steve said. "Comes of

being right ninety-nine percent of the time. He gets to thinking he's infallible, and if you disagree, watch out."

"If he shouts, you're safe enough," Chuck said. "It's when he's quiet you've got to cover your ass."

I thought of the tantrum over the robot costume and made it four Sunday Breakfast Specials. Maybe the sausage wouldn't be cold this morning. Fat chance.

"Say," Rich said. "It's a gruesome way to start the day, but I've heard some rumors about a murder."

Suddenly, I was the resident expert.

Back in the room, I called Karen. She answered sleepily, as I'd expected. It wasn't quite nine o'clock.

"Bad news, Kay," I told her.

"Oh, no," she said, wide awake. "Is somebody dead?"

I suppose, given previous experience, she had reason to jump to that conclusion. And, given the present situation, I could scarcely resent it.

"Yes."

Silence on the line for a few seconds. "This time there wasn't even a UFO," she said. "Who was it? Maureen what's-her-name?"

"Maureen? No. Why her?"

"Oh, she just struck me as somebody who likes to live a little closer to the edge than might be good for her."

"No, she's okay as far as I know," I said. "But as a matter of fact it was the guy who was with her Friday night. Name of Cassius Grenzman. He was playing Killer, and somebody shot him." But where *is* Maureen? I wondered.

"You weren't there, I hope," said my wife.

"No, of course I wasn't there."

"But you found the body."

"No. Mack and another cop found him. We were talking on the stairs and heard a shot—"

"You *were* there."

124

"Three floors away," I protested.

"Wait till Prunella Watson hears this," Karen said. "You don't even have to have the UFO. All you have to do is start talking."

"Quit that!" I snapped. "You sound like Mack. And Prunella"—a sweet old lady with two yellow cats who had founded her organization in hope of catching an alien in the act, and chosen the name to match—"won't be entertained at all."

More silence, then a sigh. "I'm sorry, Joe," Karen said. "But it does seem like UFOs get you involved in an awful lot of violence, doesn't it? Most people go through their whole lives without ever seeing anybody get really hurt, let alone murdered, but you—What is this now, eight? And you're not even a cop!"

"Karen, there's nothing I can do about it."

"When's your panel discussion?"

"Eleven-thirty."

"Do you want me to come?" she asked. In the background, I heard Joey call her.

"If you're interested," I said.

"Well, I'll see how it goes," she said. In other words, no. "Joe, I've got to go. Please, be careful. How's Mack taking it?"

"Mack?"

"It's his big security job," she pointed out. "His reputation is on the line. Isn't that what he said?"

Mack's right, I thought. He'll have to find the killer, if only to keep his morale intact. As I said good-bye to Karen, I was half-wishing that Mack's business partner—the answering machine—*had* been an FBI castoff. Maybe then it would have some useful ideas about what to do next.

With two hours left before my panel discussion was scheduled to start, I went looking for Mack. No one in the con office knew where he was. I poked my head into the room across the hall where the cops had set up a field office and asked the man in uniform if he'd seen Mack Forrester, but the guy didn't know him.

Making his rounds maybe, or up in the con suite. I opted for the latter and got onto the elevator with four Klingons, a cave girl whose mate had slain two or three very small animals at most, and a dog approximately the size of a Shetland pony. The Klingons were trying not to leer at the girl, who belonged to the dog. My young Klingon friend of the night before wasn't among them.

At the door to the con suite Michelle the Vulcan was badging, this time clad in a *gi* tied with a black belt and frilly pink slippers.

"The college boys must have made quite an impression on you," I said as she nodded me in.

"No, it's more like I'm hoping to make a few impressions on them," she said.

"Oh?"

"Fists, fingers, feet, they're all good for making impressions," she explained, grinning. "Teach them to keep their hands off."

I grinned back. "You seen Mack?" I asked.

"Not this morning," she said. The grin vanished. "Hey, what's going on?" she asked. "You wouldn't believe what I'm hearing. Cass Grenzman was killed last night. Did you know? The cops talked to all the badgers and the security volunteers. I'd just gone to bed and they got me up. Four o'clock! Did they do that to everybody?"

"Not me," I said. "They got to me earlier."

"Lucky you." Michelle stood on the rungs of the stool to see whether a sleepy fan had a badge as he entered. "They asked me every question they could think of, but they didn't say a word about what happened. Do you know?"

I nodded. "He was into a game of Killer. Somebody was

playing with real bullets. Mack and I and a couple of the rent-a-cops were on the scene a few seconds later, but it was too late to do anything for him. That's about all I know."

"Oh, that's why they had Marie listen in on the game." Michelle nodded at another pink badge and glanced behind her. "Was his body really covered with satanist symbols traced in blood?" she asked in a low voice.

"No."

Her shoulders rose and sank under the loose white pajamas. "That's a relief," she said. "I s'pose there wasn't a white holly stake through his heart, either, though *that* I could understand. You're sure he was shot?"

I nodded again.

"That's a bigger relief." She met my eyes soberly. "I'd heard he was kicked."

I glanced down at her belt.

"Not me, Marie. Though I guess what goes for her goes for me, too," she added reflectively. "I was as mad as she was, I can tell you that."

"What happened?"

"Let's just say, he gave her a hard time Friday night. You know about the skinny-dipping?"

"I hear it's a tradition at cons."

Michelle nodded once, vigorously. "Cass had to be asked to leave the pool area Friday. Marie wasn't the only one. . . ." Her voice trailed off as she looked after someone who had just come into the room. "Friend? May I see your badge, please?"

At least it will keep him away from the pool, Yates had said. Not disinterested. Mildly disgusted. How many people besides the twins had Grenzman enraged?

"Is Marie a black belt, too?" I asked.

She glanced back at me. "Of course. We're clones, you know," she said.

127

"Clones?"

But now it was Jack Ferraro coming through the door, his hand raised to clap me on the shoulder and a big smile on his face. Michelle glanced at his badge and accosted the badgeless girl trying to shelter behind him, so I abandoned the conversation.

"Glad to see you, J.J.," Ferraro said as he headed for the tray of doughnuts on a table under the window. "You heard about Cass? I'd like to find out what's going on...."

Once again, I was the resident expert.

"I wonder ...," Ferraro said, about ten minutes later. "No. Can't be."

"What?"

He grimaced slightly and jerked his head. "I was wondering if all those pranks were a setup for Grenzman's murder. Some kind of warning, or just working up to it. But I don't think so."

I'd gone through last night's story in a fair amount of detail, not having been told in so many words to keep my mouth shut, and Ferraro had sat staring out at the Metrodome for three or four minutes after I'd run down. Now he gulped the rest of what must have been frigid coffee and shook his head decisively. "No, I think Grenzman was doing the pranks," he said. "And that's what killed him. Somebody took exception to having the con done in."

"Why would Grenzman try to do in the con?"

"You had to know the guy," Ferraro said. "Vicious bastard. If he took a dislike to you, you really had to watch your step. You've talked to Mack Forrester. You must know Grenzman was dead set—sorry—against the security here."

"Yeah, but what's so vicious about a few firecrackers and some fraternity boys?"

"Money."

"Hold on." I picked up his cup and my own and made a

trip to the coffee urn. "Okay. How does money get involved here?" I asked, sitting down again.

"Once a con gets going, there's a balance from year to year," Ferraro explained. "It's a business. Doesn't matter how starry eyed the organizers are, if it's gonna keep going it's got to run like any other business. It's got to make a profit." He was just warming up: he crouched over the table and started gesturing with long, tanned hands.

"Look at all the people a big con has to pay," he continued. "The hotel, printers, a lawyer, insurance, security, advertising space. That's just off the top of my head. Who knows what else? But believe me, there are bills. And some of them have to be paid well in advance, so you can't count on your preregistrations and the huckster-space rent to carry you through. For the deposits, you use last year's profit, see?"

"Sure."

"But this is the *first* year for Twin-Con. Most cons start small and work up, so they don't have the cash-flow problems this one does, but these guys wanted to start out with something big. The money came out of the organizers' own pockets—some of them, that is. Bascombe took out an equity loan on his house, for example. The guy's thirty years old and walks around looking like a weekend yuppie, but he's really just a janitor in an elementary school. How's he going to pay that loan back if the con goes under?"

"Mmmm."

"He could lose his house," Ferraro said. "And any chance of getting another one for a good long while—with the baby on the way. . . . "

"Yeah, I can see how that might complicate things," I agreed.

"He's not the only one that would be in trouble, either. You've met Sue Evers? Redheaded woman with a long neck? Looks like the queen of Shangri-la?"

"Yeah."

"*She* took out a pretty hefty bank loan. She's just started her own business, that new fabric store in Linden Hills, and she used that for collateral. I was on the small-business aid committee that helped her plan the shop, and I guarantee you she's not figuring to declare bankruptcy in her first six months!" He caught my skeptical glance. "Don't think she's as fragile as she looks. The woman does three tri-athalons a year and she's just as tough when it comes to business. If she thought Grenzman was doing her in, she'd be capable of anything. Then there's Rita Partridge. . . . "

By the time he got done, Ferraro had made a case for suspecting half the members of the concom on financial grounds and the other half of the concom and a dozen or more of the fans on political grounds. And he hadn't even touched on plain dislike or sudden rage.

"You haven't heard of any pranks today, have you?" he concluded.

"I just got up," I said.

"There won't be any," he predicted. "Not with Grenzman dead."

"The con's almost over," I pointed out. "Any damage is already done. Why bother with anything else?"

"You're not dealing with rationality here," Ferraro said. "Those tricks are some kind of revenge, believe it, and revenge knows no end. Grenzman was behind them, I'd bet my nose on it."

"I had another candidate for the pranks. But I guess there's no obvious motive."

"Who?"

"Donovan."

Ferraro laughed loud and long. The Klingon boy of the night before, metamorphosed to a shy teenager in jeans and a con T-shirt, had claimed a small stack of doughnuts from the tray and stood gaping at the laughing Ferraro. I raised my hand, and he came over.

I introduced him, and ten minutes later left the two of them eagerly discussing the UFOs sighted in Brazil and southern California the previous spring. The only clipping on the case in my files came from a supermarket tabloid that had also told me that John Lennon had returned to this world as a crow, so I wished them well and left them to it.

"Do you know a girl named Maureen?" I asked Michelle the Vulcan on my way out. "Concom member?"

"Sure. Everybody knows Maureen, many of your sex in several senses," she said, detaching a random two-year-old from her pants leg as its mother dashed for the dwindling supply of doughnuts.

"Have you seen her this morning?"

She gave me an I-thought-you-were-married stare and said, "No."

"What can you tell me about her?"

"Not much," Michelle said. "She likes to say she's an army brat, but I don't see why she has to drag in the army."

"I can see you're bosom buddies," I said.

Michelle smiled. "Maureen's all right. If only she wouldn't worry so much about Maureen."

"I wonder if she even knows about Grenzman?"

Michelle closed her eyes and sucked in her lips. "If she does, she's probably out celebrating," she said. "The word's going around that she and Cass broke up after she objected to the swimming pool bit. Maureen doesn't take to having her men wander."

I could believe that last. A certain kind of woman wants all the male attention in the room, and Maureen was one of them. But celebrating?

"And Cass didn't like to be tied down, though I hear Maureen might have thought she'd be the one to do it," Michelle said. She thoughtfully hitched her belt a little tighter and smoothed the ends with a kind of affection.

"She's a funny woman, Maureen. Smarter than she acts. Or used to be," she added, but didn't elaborate.

Motive upon motive. Feeling a little dizzy, I left the current hub of what Bascombe had described to me as "the friendly world of fandom" and picked up my search for Mack.

Chapter Twelve

As I approached the concom office, a high-pitched wail floated toward me. I started to run. Only a couple of yards from the office, I flinched as the door flew open and Diz Donovan darted into the hall, wild-eyed.

"What—?" I started to ask.

Donovan didn't even see me. He caromed off my left shoulder and dashed away, still screeching. I bounced against the wall and went down. The cop chasing Donovan jumped neatly over my legs, shouting, "Stop, in the name of the law!" His right hand fumbled at the holster as he ran. I'd started to get up, but plain instinct made me cringe toward the wall—a good thing; two more police officers pounded past me without a glance.

I rose to my knees, staring after them.

All four men had rounded the corner of the corridor. A wordless shout from someone told me nothing. After a moment I got to my feet, and as I did the first officer returned around the corner, marching Donovan ahead of him with Diz sobbing in a peculiar staccato soprano.

"Better get out of the way," Mack said from behind me.

I ducked into the concom office, jaw still sagging. The old woman with the cat was back, both of them dozing in the big chair as if nothing much were happening, and a young, thin man wearing a dark gray business suit and yellow paisley tie paced savagely across the back of the room.

Donovan got his articulation back, enough so that I could make out, "I didn't, I didn't do it, I didn't, you got to listen to me, I didn't...."

"What's going on?" I asked.

"He's being taken in for questioning in the murder of Cassius Grenzman," Mack said. His deadpan expression made the hair on the back of my neck rise.

"Thank God! Now that we've got that fiend out of here, maybe we can begin getting back to normal!" With his voice, I recognized the pacing man as the hotel manager I'd seen on TV two nights before. He put two fingers to each side of his forehead and closed his eyes; brown circles under them advertised his problems of the past two days. "That man Bascombe seemed so sane," he complained, moving his head from side to side. "And Miss Evers. I had no idea . . . " The manager trailed off, and out of the room.

"He's calmed down some," Mack remarked, closing the door after him. "Last night he was going to have my P.I. license yanked, and maybe see my U.S. citizenship canceled."

Out in the hall, one of the cops was reading Donovan his rights. Whether the man could make any sense of them over his own lamentations seemed an open question. But something did get through.

The keening changed to, "I'll die in jail, you can't put me in jail, I'll die there, you know I will, it's plain murder . . . " His voice got fainter as he was led away. The last thing I heard was, "They'll feed me *white bread!*"

Mack snorted.

"Donovan killed Grenzman?" I asked. The room seemed eerily silent.

"They think," Mack said.

"And you?"

He shook his head. "They've got the wrong man. For all the right reasons, but the wrong man. Sit down and have a doughnut, I'll tell you about it."

I refused the doughnut and accepted some coffee—not Vulcan, by the lack of flavor. Only one of the headsets was on the table. A nearly full security crew must be working.

"What Donovan did do was pull all those pranks," Mack said, mouth full. "Seen the paper?"

"This morning's? Not yet."

Mack tossed the front section toward me. "Story starts on the front page. Inside, they talk about all the stuff's gone wrong here and quote the Chief of Police as asking any citizen with any pertinent information to come forward."

"Yeah, that's his line," I said, scanning the first paragraphs, which were much what I would have expected, given the haste with which they must have been written. "Crimes are solved and/or prevented by nosy old ladies. I've heard the guy say it at least half a dozen times."

Mack glanced at the woman in the chair, whose mouth had dropped open to emit a delicate snore. "And he's right," he said. "Half the time, anyway. Something like this, maybe even ninety percent of the time."

"Sure." I turned to page six and finished a somewhat scanty report of the pranks. Mack finished his doughnut.

"So they had two calls this morning," he continued. "One from a kid in the apartment house where Donovan lives, who said Donovan paid him to distribute the flyers over at the University. He was supposed to paper all those little colleges in Saint Paul, too, but he never got there."

"Donovan paid him?" I repeated stupidly.

"What the hell did I just say?" Mack snapped. He shook his head and yawned, pinching the bridge of his nose. "Sorry. Didn't mean that. The other call was from a 7-Eleven store a couple of blocks from where Donovan lives. He bought a dozen boxes containing eight utility candles each only last week. The manager remembers because she made him pay cash—he's a regular customer, and he bounced a check on her a few weeks back—and because there were only three boxes on the shelf and she had to send a clerk into the back room to hunt up the rest. Meanwhile, he carried on about the rotten way she ran the store and so on—you know how he does." Mack yawned. "Now they'll run around and show his picture in all the X-rated video stores."

"Okay, so he did the pranks," I said, reaching for a sweaty-looking chocolate doughnut after all. "What's that got to do with the murder?"

"Remember that argument you reported to me, secondhand?"

"Yeah."

"At the end of it, in front of half a dozen witnesses, Donovan told Grenzman that people—Donovan said 'specimens,' check?—like him should be exterminated, and this time when he talked Grenzman had better pay attention."

"Unh." That would do it.

"Seems they've had an ongoing disagreement for months about weapons policy and whether people should be allowed to play Killer. Naturally all kinds of other stuff got dragged in, you know how it goes. I hear it got pretty hot at times. And the last couple of days Grenzman has been questioning Donovan's sanity, aloud and in public . . . you can imagine why. He's a flake, all right."

"Flake, yes, but somehow I don't see Donovan firing a gun," I mused.

"As a matter of fact, neither do I, but that means zip. It doesn't take much. Anybody with one good hand and a vengeful attitude is in business."

"Good, good," said the old woman, opening her eyes. Mack gawked at her. "About vengeance, I mean," she explained. "As motivation. But it obeys the transitive law, if I'm not mistaken. Don't forget that."

"Transitive law?" Mack echoed.

"I think she means that you can take vengeance on behalf of somebody else," I said.

"Bright boy. You'll go far," the woman said, with rather more sarcasm than I liked. "Although primary considerations are more likely to engage the emotions."

"Check," Mack said in a fainter voice than usual.

"As in poor Desmond's case. I know he was very worried about what Cassius might have said to that nice engineer. I told him if he did his job well, nobody would care what some stranger said." The woman struggled out of the chair, tottered a moment, and steadied herself.

"Cass was talking to some engineer about Diz?" Mack asked.

"Or Desmond thought he was. It's hard to tell. You'll have to excuse me, young man. Nature calls with exasperating frequency as one ages." She hitched the cat onto her shoulder. "Still, one must never close one's mind too quickly, you must remember that. Other possibilities come to mind," she added, and shuffled out, leaving the door standing open.

"What the hell was that about?" Mack asked when the old woman was safely out of earshot.

"Got me."

"Think she knows something?"

"Maybe. Maybe not."

"Let's hope not. And let's hope she doesn't go around talking like that to any- and everyone. Unless, of course, I'm wrong about Donovan, though I have to agree he's the best-looking prospect I can see at the moment."

Running footsteps sounded in the hall. Mack half-stood. Bascombe swung into the room, grabbing at the doorjamb for a brake. "Forrester, what the hell's going on?" he asked, panting. "Diz was arrested for killing Cass?"

Mack plopped back down. "Not arrested. Held for questioning. They haven't charged him."

"They can't *do* that! How can they do that?"

For a moment, Mack looked as if he were about to quote the appropriate section of the law. Instead, he said, "You heard about that argument yesterday, just before lunch?"

"Sure, it went on off and on all day, but hell, it was only an argument." Bascombe, beginning to breathe more evenly, sat down and automatically reached for the doughnut box. "Mack, you know as well as I do that Diz couldn't kill anybody. He's a vegetarian, for Christ's sake!"

"Even vegetarians get angry," Mack pointed out. "Sometimes angry enough to kill."

"Mack, if they arrested everybody who ever had an argument with Cass Grenzman, half the con would be in jail, and a hell of a lot of other people besides."

"But Cass was right," Mack said. "Maybe Diz was afraid he had proof to back up what he said."

"Proof!" Bascombe pushed the empty box away. "Proof of what?"

"That Diz was your prankster."

"Diz?" Bascombe's face, flushed with rage a moment before, went white. He looked from Mack to me and back to Mack, and swallowed twice. "Not Diz. Oh, no. Couldn't be Diz. I'm sure it was Cass. Had to be."

"There's proof it was Diz, two independent witnesses so far, and he admits it," Mack said. He sat back and folded his arms, head on one side.

"But I've known Diz since high school," Bascombe pleaded. "We aren't real buddies, but we always get along. Always. Hell, we read the same stuff, we like the same music! Why would he do something like that to me?"

"That I can't tell you," Mack said. "You'll have to ask him."

"He'll just say nobody pays attention to him," Bascombe said with a quick, dismissive gesture, as if he'd crumpled a sheet of paper and tossed it aside. "Which isn't true. Anyway, what does that have to do with murder?"

Mack shifted. "Diz did threaten Grenzman," he said, almost gently. "And, like I said, maybe Grenzman had some kind of proof that Diz was sabotaging the con. You think

138

he'd want to be found out? In front of his friends?"

"No . . . no." Bascombe ran his hands through his hair, leaving the black curls standing awry. "Look, he'll need an attorney," he said. "I—maybe the guy who's working on the con—I'd better go find out if he's got one."

He got to his feet as stiffly as the old woman had done.

"If not Diz Donovan, who?" Mack asked.

Bascombe cast him a white-eyed glance. "Talk to you later," he said and walked out of the room.

"What if he's right?" I asked Mack. "You didn't think Diz killed Grenzman either, so what about other people? According to my friend Ferraro, just about everybody in the building had some reason for knocking off Grenzman."

"You trust that guy Ferraro?"

"Sure." I tried to keep my sudden discomfort out of my face.

Mack eyed me. "Strikes me he does a lot of pumping for info for a disinterested bystander. What do you s'pose he wants to know all that for?"

"No pumping this time," I assured him. "All I did was listen."

"After you spilled everything you knew."

"Mack, he *knows* these people. Some of them for years."

Mack poured us each another cup of the insipid coffee. "In that case, start talking," he ordered.

By the time I was done, I was damn near late for the panel discussion. Ferraro was on the panel, too, along with the earnest medievalist from the SCA and four other people, none of whom I'd ever seen before. I searched the audience, but couldn't see Karen. She must have got hung up, I decided. Chuck Kowalski, pink badge and all, waved at me from a middle row. I grinned back and turned my attention to Bascombe's opening remarks.

The guy looked as if he'd been up all night, which he

139

probably had, and the crisp, witty delivery of yesterday afternoon failed him. He mentioned something about "our tragedy," and how Cass would want the con to go on, and finally meandered to a stop and sat down only to bounce back up because he'd forgotten to introduce the panelists. I discovered that two of the others were science fiction writers, one a UFO enthusiast from Madison, Wisconsin, and the fourth a member of the Minnesota Skeptics, who gave each of the rest of us a bland, assessing stare. She seemed to be the only one who had brought her mind along this morning. The rest of us were no better off than Bascombe.

Nonetheless, we panelled. The audience, large to begin with, diminished steadily, and by the end of our hour we were left with a hard core of the curious, the skeptical, and the ufonuts. After the discussion petered out, Chuck came forward to say hello.

"Got me a badge without you," he said.

"From Diz?"

"No, I just buttonholed somebody on his way out the front door and borrowed the badge for a couple of hours. Couldn't find you or Diz."

"You don't know about him, then?"

"Something up?"

"He's being held for questioning."

"You're kidding! For what?"

"There was a murder here last night. Remember?"

"Jeez!" Chuck's blue eyes actually seemed to bulge. "You're not telling me Diz Donovan's been arrested for murder!"

I shrugged.

"J.J., you know as well as I do Diz is no murderer."

"I don't know him that well."

"I do."

I told him about the pranks that had been pulled on the

con and how Donovan had been linked to them.

"Yeah, I can see that," Chuck said, pulling at his lower lip with a frown. "He's a funny guy. He's real sensitive on the topic of getting his share of attention. No, I shouldn't say that. More like respect. And practical jokes are right up his alley. He'll make life hell for anybody who treats him like an idiot—not that he doesn't bring it on himself."

"Maybe this time he went a little too far?"

"Not Diz." Chuck shook his head. "I don't even quite believe that bit about stuffing the towels in the ovens. He'd never do anything to endanger life or limb. The only way that could happen is if he didn't think it all the way through." I thought of the metal tray under the fuse of the firecrackers.

One of the ufonuts had been dancing at the edge of my vision while Chuck and I talked. "You need the john, buddy?" Chuck asked him.

The guy gave him a surly glance and circled to stand behind Chuck and stare at me.

"Look, I'm going to go talk to the cops," Chuck said. "They've got to have the wrong man. Interesting panel, by the way," he added, already backing away up the aisle.

Chuck broke into a jog as the ufonut cornered me against the dais and began haranguing me about some sighting in Montana ten or twelve years ago. "This one is decisive," he informed me. "Even a horse saw it." The guy was just getting into stride when he glanced down and stopped. "Uh," he said, more of a breath than a word, and pointed.

Projecting from beneath the skirt of the dais was a finger. Or, to be more precise, the tip of a finger and the end of a long, gold-lacquered nail. I closed my eyes, certain I'd just learned what had happened to Maureen Tesla.

"We'd better . . . ," the ufonut said. "Uh, we'd better, um, we, uh, what should we do?"

"I'll stay here," I said. "You run and grab Dan Bascombe and bring him back."

"Oh, thanks," the guy said inanely and ran for the door of the conference room, where several people were still talking. I saw him snag Bascombe by the elbow, point in my direction, and leave the room with his head down. Bascombe, looking puzzled, ambled down the aisle toward me.

"What's up?" he asked.

"There's a body under here," I said.

Bascombe came to stand beside me and looked down. His face seemed to sag over his bones, and he knelt suddenly. I thought his knees had given way and reached down to steady him, but he planted a hand on the floor and picked up the skirt of the dais to look under it.

After a moment he sat back on his heels and looked up at me with a bewildered frown. "It's April," he half-whispered. "It's April Thorney."

I glanced at the room. A small knot of people chatted near the door, and at the other side of the dais the girl from the Minnesota Skeptics gestured energetically as she spoke to the medievalist and one of the writers.

"My God," Bascombe muttered. "All the while we were sitting up there, she was lying here."

Kneeling myself, I lifted the dais skirt and looked under. April, all right. I swallowed my rebelling doughnut. She had been in that warm, dark place long enough to become somewhat unpleasant.

"Have you got your headset?" I asked Bascombe.

He extended it toward me, somewhat green around the gills himself. "Can you believe this? April! It just doesn't make any sense. Cass, now, I can understand that, there've been times with Cass if I'd had a gun in my hand it might have been me shooting, but April?"

His square, stubby hand around the radio focused the fleeting memory I'd had the day before. He'd set up something to "tape" my talk—could he have been actually broadcasting to someone who'd turn off the lights at just the right moment? Himself? And then a quick dash down the two corridors with a flashlight—anyone who met him wouldn't question that he was there. Concom members were allowed where others would be off-limits.

No time for that now. I thumbed the radio on and called for Mack.

"What's up?" he demanded. "And how did you get on our network?"

"Never mind," I said. "Just come to conference room D as fast as you can. We've found the missing knife."

"Good for you," Mack said. "Don't touch it, check?"

"I wouldn't lay a finger on it, Mack," I replied. "It's been used."

Chapter Thirteen

MACK LIFTED THE heavy blue skirt of the speakers' platform for the three seconds required to be sure April Thorney was beyond mortal assistance, and dropped it, tight-mouthed.

"I called the police already," he said to Bascombe. "You'd better go meet them at the escalator and bring them back here. Meanwhile"—he glanced at the trio at the other side of the dais, still locked in earnest conversation—"I'll clear the room."

Bascombe, head down and looking thinner than he had on Friday night, went up the aisle at a trot while Mack moved over to the three remaining members of the panel and said something I didn't hear. Whatever it was couldn't have included the reason he wanted them to leave, because after a few more exchanges all three smiled affably and began strolling toward the door, unhurried. Mack returned to my side of the platform and sat heavily in the front row, forearms resting on his knees and his hands clasped between them. "They'll be around," he said "Planning to stay for the closing ceremonies. They didn't know of anything unusual going on, so I told them we need the room for another function. That always seems to get them moving. Cooperative damn crowd, in some ways."

I plopped myself down one chair away from Mack. The ventilators were sighing. I remembered how comforting that sound had been when the lights went out—while the knife was being stolen. A chill traveled slowly down my back.

"Commando style, that's what the papers will say," Mack remarked. "Must have grabbed her from behind, hand over her mouth, and stuck it right into her carotid artery. Commando style, street-tough style, TV-adventure style, call it what you want to."

"She can't have been killed here, then," I said.

"Not from what I see."

"Whoever put her under there must have been in a hurry, to leave the tip of her finger showing," I commented.

"Maybe it wasn't showing when he left," Mack said. "When I let the skirt drop, it didn't show anymore. Cloth could have been caught on it just so, could have jiggled when somebody got on the platform." He lifted his head and gazed blankly at the wall, swallowed a couple of times, and let his head drop again. "God, Joe," he half-whispered. "I killed her."

Mack hasn't called me Joe since sixth grade. I could *see* the hair raising on my forearms. "What?"

"I killed her. Me and my big mouth, last night. I told them the cops would be talking to everybody."

He stopped talking as a small party of men and one woman came into the room with Bascombe, swinging the door shut behind them. "Howdy, Forrester, what's up?" said the first of the men, extending a hand.

Mack dragged himself to his feet and shook it. A detective, I guessed, but not the one I knew. This guy was as big as Mack, honey-haired and tight of gut and dressed like a Sunday Dayton's ad: slick.

Mack pasted a hasty polite smile on his face. "Hi, Sergeant." His voice seemed under control. "We found our dragon knife, as J.J. puts it," he said, with a jerk of his head at me.

Thanks, I thought.

"You two stay put," the detective said. "Let me get a look at this place and get organized. The body's where?"

146

"Under the platform," Bascombe said, pointing.

"Okay. You were called to the scene after it was discovered, am I right?"

Bascombe nodded, looking at me.

"You touch anything?"

Amazing how shifty an honest man can sometimes look. "I—I picked up the, the cloth and looked under," Bascombe said.

"Stooping or kneeling?"

"Uh—kneeling, I think."

"Anything else?"

Bascombe shook his head.

"Daniel Robert Bascombe, isn't it? You can go for now, but don't leave the hotel. I'll want to talk to you later. Can we lock that door?"

"I'll find out."

"Jamison, you found the body?"

"Er . . . yes. There was a ufonut talking to me—"

"A what?"

"Ufonut. Somebody nuts on UFOs."

"Name?"

"Dunno. His badge said he was Krashisha of Kark."

"Christ." The detective sergeant rolled his eyes. "Where is he now?"

"I sent him to get Bascombe and he disappeared."

"Next time put a leash on him," the detective said and walked away with a gesture to me to stay where I was.

He spent the next few minutes organizing a search of the scene. Nobody so much as lifted the skirt of the platform. A flash marked the first of what would be many photographs, this one taken of the dais from a distance. The detective nodded with satisfaction. While one of the other men began making a sketch plan of the room, the detective came over and sat down next to Mack and started asking questions: some Mack answered and some he

147

referred to me. In perhaps five minutes we'd covered the discovery of the body, a bit of April Thorney's background, and the gist of what Mack knew of events the night before. He didn't mention his speech in the concom office, and neither did I.

"We'll have to go back through all these weirdos and find out when she was last seen alive," the detective said finally, tapping his pencil eraser against his teeth. "Christ, I don't look forward to that."

"I saw her around eleven last night," I said.

"Ah?"

"There was a costume contest. They gave her a special prize." I told him why and suddenly found myself closely questioned, first about the episode in the con suite with the three drunks and then about the contest—who had thought of the prize, who had done the lettering, who had sculpted the medal, who the judges were, who had won what the detective called the 'legit awards.'

"Bascombe is the man you want to ask about that," I protested, looking around for the concom chair, but he had already left.

"I dunno how to say this," the detective said, "but did you notice any unusual incidents at the contest? Allowing for where we are."

"Diz Donovan threw a tantrum," I said.

I found Mack looking at me somewhat oddly.

"Ah," my questioner said. "Tell me more about that."

I did. "So Donovan had a motive for killing this broad, too," the detective concluded.

"Over a costume contest?" Mack asked. "It's not as if she took any prizes away from him—"

"Listen," the detective interrupted. "I just came from two hours of talking to that s.o.b. and I'm here to tell you he doesn't think like you and me, or anybody else you or I ever met. He's in jail on suspicion of homicide, and all he could talk about was some damn fake robot he left here."

"His costume," Mack said.

Once again, the hair on the back of my neck lifted. I folded my hands over my forearms. The fake robot was big enough for Donovan, a fairly tall, angular man, to climb into and be concealed. Not only that, it was wide-based, to give it a low center of gravity—somewhat wider than needed just to contain Diz. Could a short, fat woman fit into it? I glanced at Mack and kept quiet.

A burst of motion at the speakers' platform ended with a series of loud zips as one of the men stripped the skirt from its Velcro fastening. Revealed, the substructure of the platform showed it to be several large, heavy-duty folding tables locked together. The body lay sprawled on its back, one arm outflung, with all the grace of a sack of potatoes fallen off a truck. The haft of the polished silver knife, still lodged under the angle of the jaw, caught the light like a monstrous piece of jewelry. Mack and the detective looked toward the sudden activity.

Mack cleared his throat. "Never get any decent prints off that knife handle," he said.

"Why?"

"It's something like those no-fingerprint panels they put on refrigerators. Supposed to be flames, though from the picture I saw it looks to me more like dragon scales."

So the knife, artwork though it might be, had its utilitarian aspects as well. Perhaps the choice had been dictated by its sharpness and the print-proof handle and not by the beauty of the etched dragon at all. In that case, I wondered whether the police would catch this killer. Anyone who could seize upon circumstances and make a plan that quickly would be slippery as hell. If he had, in fact, made it that quickly.

"Might get something off her skin," the detective commented. "Joanna? Make sure that face doesn't get touched! You're gonna be looking for fingermarks, or bruises."

The woman nodded, still hanging back from the scene. I wondered who she was. She wasn't helping the men with their search, which progressed slowly outward from the platform.

"Here's something," said one of them. The photographer and the other searcher joined him, looking at something on the floor. "Blood, maybe."

The man who had found the blood got out of the way as the photographer placed a camera in a frame over the spot and took two pictures. That done, the first man dropped to one knee, chalked a circle on the floor, and opened a measuring tape. When he extended it, the end of the tape struck the back wall to the right of the exit door. Everyone looked at it but no one said anything. The photographer squeezed off a shot and the man measuring wrote something on a report form.

As the evidence men continued putzing with their possible drop of blood, I slid down in my chair as much as I dared, looking for wheel tracks across the hard-twist carpet, but saw nothing... unless that was a part of a mark near the platform. From where I was, I couldn't tell, and I couldn't move closer to examine it. Glancing at Mack, I saw only a blank face.

"Killed somewhere else and brought through that door, maybe," one of the searchers said. "Where does the door go?"

"Service corridor," Mack said.

"Want us to rope that off, too, Sergeant?"

"Right. Where do you go from the corridor, Forrester?"

Mack lifted his hands helplessly. "With connections, anywhere in the hotel."

"She's a pretty big lady," one of the men remarked. "You think she was carried?"

150

"Not far," said the other.

"I saw some laundry carts downstairs last night that might do the trick," the first one said. "We'd better check them out."

But would there even be wheel marks? I took a slow survey of the room, saw a few crush marks where chairs had been moved, and concluded that it wasn't impossible. The robot itself must weigh at least a hundred pounds and April would have added another two hundred.

The detective sergeant wrote something in his notebook and sat stroking his jaw a moment. He glanced at me, as if he'd forgotten I was there, and said, "Okay, Jamison. Out of here."

I didn't have to be told twice. "Hang around and when Joy picks me up we'll give you a ride home, check?" Mack offered, as I got to my feet.

"Sure," I said, knowing an order when I heard one, no matter who gave it. One of the officers trailed me to the double door of the conference room and let me out. In the reception area the sf fans carried on as if nothing had happened.

But then, I doubt that any of them knew what the unscheduled event in conference room D had turned out to be.

"Okay, poker-face," Mack said. "I saw the bulb light up over your head. Give."

Two-thirty. The con was officially over at four. In the huckster room most of the booksellers were already packing up. Many of the fans had left, their names and addresses registered with the police. I'd called Karen and, coward that I am, told her only that Mack had offered me a ride home, and I'd probably stay the afternoon. She'd apologized for missing the panel, saying she had some ideas that had to be written down right away. I'd thought of

151

the chrysanthemums beside the house on the corner. They'd be as golden as their name implied today, the rough glittery stone wall beneath them seamed with a grayish plant I'd never stopped to look at closely. Turning back into the stale hotel light had been hard, even though I could console myself that picnics were unlikely to be on the schedule with Karen scribbling.

Now, rather oddly, Mack and I had the Wellesford Regal's salad bar to ourselves, with the exception of a well-rounded old lady in a magenta felt hat. Perhaps lunch in a hotel where a man had been killed the night before didn't strike the downtown crowd as an appropriate post-church activity. Mack had stowed away a prodigious amount of greenery, well-laced with ham and cheese, and I'd managed to choke down a turkey sandwich.

"Donovan's robot," I said.

"Wheel marks?"

"No. Just speculation."

Mack stared into the distance for a minute or two, working at a piece of something stuck in his teeth with his tongue. "That would narrow it down," he said.

"What do you mean?"

"Staff vacuums that room around six in the morning," he said. "On that twist carpet, if there'd been any wheel marks, they'd have been erased. And the blood"—he stopped and brushed his hand over his forehead to erase a momentary furrowing—"well, I got a look at that. One small drop, sunk between the twists. You know what the housekeeping's like here. Whoever ran the vacuum wouldn't have seen it in a million years. So if the robot was used to move her—and for my money that's a hell of a lot more likely than some damn laundry cart—she was put under the platform sometime before six this morning. But where was she in the meantime? The assistant M.E. says she was probably killed between midnight and two. That's

152

a guess, of course, but she wouldn't make it if she didn't think it was likely."

She. Joanna. The woman must be the assistant medical examiner, explaining why she didn't take part in the search. "Did they find any more blood?" I asked.

"They're searching the rooms now."

"Nothing in the service corridor?"

"One lousy drop, right outside the conference room." I got a one-sided grin. "I see you're thinking like me. Along that corridor to the other one, then up or down anywhere in the service elevator. The way I calculate it, that thing should just about fit through the door beside the elevator on each floor."

"Mack, the robot was standing out last night, remember? In the middle of that space at the top of the escalators. I saw it before Grenzman got shot, and it was still there after you checked the huckster room."

Mack frowned. "Or there again."

"It's the nosy-old-lady factor again," I said. "What we need is to find some busybody who saw it moving around early this morning."

Mack gave me his pitying look. "You haven't caught on to these guys yet, have you? *Anybody* could move that thing, and nobody would bat an eye. Fifty people could have shoved it around, alone or in teams, and nobody else would think twice."

"One thing I do know," I said. "It knocks out the idea that Donovan didn't kill Grenzman."

"It does?"

"What? Somebody came to him and said, 'Hey, Diz, I just stuck a knife in April and I need your robot to hide her body, can I have it awhile?' And he says, 'Sure?' You'd believe that?"

The waiter, a different old man from the morning before, but with the identical tired shuffle, dropped off a check at the elderly woman's table and came past to refill our coffee cups and favor us with a mournful stare. We'd been there a while. Mack waited until he had shuffled away to the cashier's desk and had started to chat before answering.

"Even assuming that the same person killed both of them, you're forgetting something, J.J. Diz didn't get first prize in the costume contest. You told Sergeant Ashe about his tantrum yourself."

"So?"

"So he wasn't particularly interested in the thing last night. He didn't want it until this morning."

"After he remembered it was full of blood!"

"After he remembered it. Period. The thing was essentially up for grabs from eleven last night on. Like you just said, we saw it sitting in the second-floor reception lounge ourselves."

The cashier said something to the waiter, who nodded and went behind the screen that kept us plebeians from observing any untidiness where the coffee and the water pitchers lived. He emerged, shuffling, with one of the latter in his hand.

"So you think somebody grabbed it. That narrows the field to the same five hundred people as before," I said.

"Uh-uh." Mack shut his eyes for a moment, and I remembered what he had said about the people in the concom office. "I'm ready to believe that the same guy who stole the knife used it," he said, "and that couldn't have been Donovan. Not if he was turning out the lights."

"But you don't *know* that Donovan was turning out the lights."

"He said so."

"Sure. Wouldn't you? He may be crazy, but crazy doesn't mean you can't think."

The waiter drifted slowly toward us. The invisible people of the world, I thought, mailmen and maids and waiters

154

who water the long planters full of palm trees and philodendrons out of ice water pitchers, leaving the management to wonder why the plants all die. Mack chewed his mustache, frowning.

"Shutting the lights off matches the rest," he said. "All but the linen in the ovens and the open refrigerators. Those I can't believe Diz did, 'specially the refrigerators. You've heard his views on food."

"You've got two pranksters, then," I pointed out. "How are you going to sort out who did what?"

Mack pondered that for several seconds and shrugged.

"Mack, what you said before, that it had to be one of the people in that room last night." He winced. "Donovan was there."

"So were a dozen other people."

"None of them very likely, if you ask me."

"J.J., you've got no imagination," Mack said. "Not cop-type. *Anybody* can be likely, given the right circumstances. Me. You. The Luger lady."

"I see your point," I said. "But as far as this goes, the only other one I can make any argument for is Bascombe. He was on the scene lickety-split last night, and he's my candidate for the lights." I told Mack about the purported tape recorder. "So he could have timed it perfectly. And nobody would wonder if they caught him in the service corridor, because he's got a perfect right to be there."

Mack thought about that for a moment or two, blinking somberly at the place setting the waiter had neglected to remove from the far side of the table when we sat down. "I can't see any of it," he complained, turning his coffee cup to study its empty bottom. "I can't make any scenarios. There's too much I don't know—for example, what April thought of Diz."

"I know what April thought of Diz," I said. "Friday night they were on friendly terms, and yesterday morning I saw him in the huckster room, helping her pick out some kind of gadget to stick in her hair. Both of them smiling."

"Mmm." Mack pulled as morose a face as I've ever seen on him. "Yeah. That's not good. See, whoever knifed her had to be somebody she thought she could trust, or she wouldn't have turned her back. Ah, hell, I'm forgetting, myself. These are sf fans. Bunch of trusting damn souls. Half of them make sure not to lock the doors of their rooms. Tape the latches, can you beat that?"

Not offhand. "Fascinating," I said. "What for?"

"So anybody can crash."

Logical. "What about last night?" I asked. "Is that all sewn up? I mean, as far as physical evidence goes."

"Sewn up!" Mack snorted. "They haven't even found the gun."

The waiter screamed.

The water pitcher flew into the air, bounced off the sneeze guard over the salad bar and crash-landed in the pickled beets. The waiter sprinted wild-eyed and still screaming into the kitchen while the cashier stood up behind her register and gaped after him. After a moment she ran to inspect the planter the man had been watering and shrieked herself, but stood her ground. She turned to us, white-faced, eyebrows on high, and pointed toward the line of palms. An assortment of odd noises came out of her mouth.

A narrow, wet, undoubtedly equally frightened face peered from between the heart-shaped leaves of the philodendrons, and after a pause a few inches of the coppery-gray dark-striped body of Kundala oozed onto the tiled edge of the planter.

"It's very timid, really," I said, with authority born of a two-minute conversation, and got up to grab the snake behind the neck while the cashier backed gratefully away. Kundala lunged toward me.

156

Eight feet of unexpected boa constrictor against one's chest is a considerable force. I sat suddenly among the ice cubes on the carpet. The woman in the magenta hat stood up and stretched her neck to see what was happening. Not wanting to disappoint her, I grinned my most fatuous grin and stroked the beast's wet body.

Slowly, slowly, it began to coil around my waist.

Chapter Fourteen

I COWERED INTO Kundala's embrace as a large, fierce man in white loomed over me, brandishing a butcher knife.

"Yoo weel hol' verr' steel," he informed me. "Me, I weel cot zee snik."

"Now, hold on," Mack said, moving into the danger area between me and the knife. "That snake's perfectly harmless."

"Ees beeg snik," said the man with the butcher knife.

He circled Mack on tiptoe toward my left, while Mack turned to guard Kundala and me from him. Mack was maybe half an inch taller than the cook, not counting the puffy white hat, and carried a few pounds more muscle. Even so, my back began to feel extraordinarily vulnerable.

"It's okay, it's okay," the cashier said breathlessly. She put a hand on the cook's muscular arm.

The elderly woman in the magenta felt hat made for the door, giving the snake, Mack, and the knife a judicious berth. She left her check and a bill on the cashier's desk, waggled her fingers at me with an inane smile of farewell, and scuttled toward freedom. I saw her bright bonnet bob past the planters that separated the restaurant from the walkway to the east wing at a remarkably respectable pace.

"The sna—" I stopped and cleared my throat. "The snake's a pet. It's harmless," I said.

"Pet?" asked the cook, his eyebrows nearly dislodging his hat. "Yoo keep heem een houss?"

"No," I said. "It's not mine. It belongs to—what's the name of that Amazon, Mack?"

"Miranda O'Shea."

"Belongs to a lady named Miranda O'Shea."

"You again!" The manager on duty, once again the beleaguered man of Friday and Saturday nights, charged through the space between planters that constituted the entrance to the restaurant. "What is it this time?" He caught sight of the snake. "Oh, you found it. That's a relief."

Mack smiled sheepishly.

"You can go back to the kitchen, Harold," the manager said.

"You sure?" the cook asked. "That thing looks awful dangerous to me."

"The snake is a valuable specimen, I'm told," the manager said, not quite managing to sound as if he believed it. "We want it alive and well."

If the manager had told him the Wellesford Regal's fanciest restaurant had just converted to a pizzeria, Harold could not have looked more baffled. But he lowered the knife, wiped both sides of the blade contemplatively on his apron, and returned to the kitchen without a backward glance.

"When am I going to get my service area back, that's what I want to know," the manager demanded, stepping toward Mack. "We're crippled without it. Don't you realize that? Tomorrow's Monday! We've *got* to be able to take deliveries. We have three restaurants to run, and we're damn near out of food after that fiasco with the refrigerators Friday night. Thanks to this bunch of crazies we're damn near out of linen, half of my staff is threatening to quit and the rest of them have to traipse through the lobby when they go off duty—"

"You'll have to take that up with—"

"—the Minneapolis Police Department," the manager chimed in, with flared nostrils. "Passing the buck, just like

160

Bascombe. There will be no science fiction convention at the Wellesford Regal next year, I guarantee you that!" His voice whined upward. "It's not bad enough they skinny-dip in the pool half the night. Do you know what my other guests think of that?"

I thought the engineers might appreciate it, but who am I to say? Besides, I had a snake to think about.

"And that's not bad enough! They've got to wander around in freak costumes and scare my other guests half to death. It's not bad enough there's beer cups all over hell and gone. It's not bad enough they come demanding Christ knows what—lunch in the Salad Bar at four in the morning, dollar postage stamps from the desk clerk in the middle of the night, Mountain Dew in the Coke machines, towels and more towels and more towels! No-o-o, I have to have a bomb scare empty out the building, tablecloths stuffed in the ovens, two thousand dollars worth of spoiled food, *and* I have to hire four off-duty cops to keep order."

"Hoo," Mack said. He sounded more tentative than he had upstairs the night before.

With reason. "Now," the manager swung on, louder, "they're killing each other off! First they paralyze my delivery area, and who can run a hotel without services? Now this afternoon I come on duty thinking thank God it's almost over and to top it all off Mattie tells me there's been another one shot or stabbed or some damn thing. Don't you people realize that conference room is booked for tonight?"

"I didn't realize that, sir, no," Mack said humbly. "I'm sure if the murderer had known, he would—"

"Now *it's* sealed off. What am I going to do about that?"

"Take it up with—"

"—the Minneapolis Police Department," the manager finished, throwing up his hands.

"I'm sorry," Mack said. "I can see your problem, but there's really nothing I can do."

161

The snake, in the course of this extended complaint, had thrown another coil around me. Having a Bi-Coloured-Python-Rock-Snake in a double-clove-hitch around my middle could have been worse, I reflected; at least I didn't have a crocodile attached to my nose. Lightly as it clasped me, I was beginning to wonder how deeply I should respect the musculature of this particular Bi-Coloured-Python-Rock-Snake, and I was tired of sitting in ice water.

"Could somebody get hold of Miranda O'Shea while I'm still able to breathe?" I inquired quickly as the manager gulped air for the next chapter of his jeremiad.

The speculation on Mack's face made me wonder. I had, after all, found a body. Two, almost. I could just see him turning a chair around, straddling the thing and folding his arms on the back, chin on his wrist while he watched the snake turn me blue. From the glance the manager gave me, he might just grab a chair of his own and join in.

Miranda O'Shea was reached through the grapevine in a finite amount of time; quite adequate, as it proved, to get me unhitched from Kundala.

"No danger," she said, laughing at me. "She's just a little scared. She thinks you're a nice, safe tree, not a mega-meal." I'd abandoned the ice water in favor of perching at the edge of a chair the cashier had brought me. Miranda squatted to my level and held out her arms. The snake flowed toward her. "Hey, she's been fed," Miranda exclaimed. "Something small. See the bulge?"

Sure enough, Kundala seemed to have a small bulge not far back of her head.

"Oh, God! Feeding my snake! I hope to hell it's something that's good for her. It's not big enough for a rat."

"Would feeding her have a calming effect?" Mack asked.

"Sure, but I have to drive to Mankato tonight, and I'd

hate to have her get carsick. Snake puke must be the all-time number one yucky substance. Stinks, too."

"Oh," Mack said.

The snake's cage hadn't been found, so Miranda casually looped thirty pounds of boa coils over one bare shoulder—she was in costume—and announced that the hotel would be missing a sheet if the box didn't turn up. Fortunately, by that time the manager had departed to lay his complaints before the police.

"Meet me in the con office when you get Kundala stowed, check?" Mack said to the girl. "Maybe we can figure out who took her and get your box back."

"Sure."

"You know, it's not a bad-looking creature, that snake," the cashier said, slipping back onto her stool. "Kind of gave me a start when I spotted it like that, though. Sorry I screamed."

"That's okay," Mack said. I had done him an injustice. He doubled the waiter's tip and paid for our lunch.

"Dollar stamps," Mack muttered, hands in his back pockets as we strolled toward the escalator. He hung back, letting Miranda O'Shea finish showing off her boa to a couple of teenagers and get on the moving stairs well ahead of us. "*Dollar* stamps. I wonder . . ." He stopped and looked around. "See any mail slots?" he asked.

"There's one near the registration desk," I said.

We walked, not fast, over to the registration desk, where Mack again stuck his hands into his back pockets in order to study the brass front of the mail drop. A slot maybe two inches tall by ten wide in a locked brass box was supplemented by a glass-fronted chute leading from the ceiling into the top of the box. The chute itself looked about four inches deep and the same ten inches wide.

"Maybe just," Mack said. "But not through the front.

Have to be dropped from upstairs." Mail wouldn't be picked up until Monday, according to the front of the box. "Hey," Mack said to the desk clerk. "Is there a box with a quicker pickup than this?"

"Sure. Outside, on the corner," the clerk said.

"Which corner?"

"Out the front door and to the right."

We went out the front door and to the right, walking faster now, and found the usual round-topped blue mailbox with a wide horizontal door on a pivot. "That's more like it," Mack said, pulling the door down to read the schedule stuck inside. "You could shove a shoebox in there, no problem. There's a pickup at four-fifteen."

"Now that we have the answer, do you mind telling me what the question is, O Karnak the Magnificent?" I demanded.

Mack smiled. "Two questions. Where is the missing gun? That's one. Two, will it fit through the slot in the mail drop? Answer, it doesn't have to."

"Ah," I said, getting it. "Mailed in the middle of the night by somebody who had to ask for stamps. Somebody in a hurry to get rid of it. Where would he, she, or it find packaging materials in the middle of the night, may I ask?"

"Trouble with you, J.J.," Mack said, "you always want to know every last damn detail. Worse than an assistant prosecutor."

I'd expected him to stalk back to the main entrance of the hotel, but instead he turned and walked away toward the alley that ran beside the north wing.

"Might as well have a look," he said. "Long as we're out here."

The alley was nothing much. The street side of the hotel had been faced with polished green marble when it was built. Three feet into the alley the cosmetics quit, leaving the solid common red brick undisguised. Macadam paved the ground from the wall of the hotel to that of the building next to it. A few miniaturized weeds had made it though the seam between tarred gravel and brick on the west side. Other than that, nothing interrupted the expanse of pavement. Mack walked into the alley, glancing from side to side.

"Almost looks swept," he commented. "Damn."

"What are you looking for?"

"Clues," he said, drawing the word out for sarcasm.

The end of the alley widened, giving plenty of room for a delivery van to turn around. Dumpsters, stuffed to overflowing with huge plastic sacks stuffed in turn with trash, lined the far side of the area. From the outside, the lift doors presented a solid brown front creased horizontally with four seams it would have been difficult to fit a knife blade into. Between the doors a bellpush was surmounted by printed instructions to ring for admittance. Next to the lift doors, the exit that had been propped open last night was shut, another flush brown surface marked only with the round brass escutcheon of a lock. Not even a knob. Mack stuck his hands in his back pockets and stared at it.

"There's another door," I said.

Mack turned to look at the other door. That one would serve the east wing as emergency exit, same as the one where Grenzman had been killed served the north wing. Mack walked over and kicked at it, but it was a twin to the first and didn't yield. Same blank face, one lock, no knob. He scratched his head and returned to the first door.

"Look at that," he said.

Nothing unusual. Several chips in the paint near the bottom of the door, of varying ages and rustiness.

"Where it was blocked open," I said.

"Thank you, Watson." The second door had no such marks. "What would you say that is between the doors," Mack asked. "Thirty feet?"

"About."

"Seven or eight running steps. Three seconds, tops."

"Unless you're on crutches."

"What I like about you, J.J. You're such a help." Mack squatted down and looked under the dumpsters and poked around beside and behind the end ones. "Ah, let's get out of here," he said. "Nothing here."

Back in the hotel, we returned to the desk to find that the clerk had not been on duty in the middle of any night, certainly not last night. What did we think he was, iron man?

Mack turned on the charm, and we left the desk possessed of the home phone number of the man who had been on duty. "Too bad you checked out already," Mack muttered, slapping the call button of the elevator with a big open hand. "I could use some privacy for this."

"Pay phone over there," I pointed out.

Mack gave it a quick glance. Like most indoor pay phones it was not enclosed. On the other hand, few people were in the lobby. He ambled over, borrowed a quarter, and made the call.

I waited, leaning against the wall as if I wanted to use the phone next, looking over the people who were in the lobby. A girl in jeans and T-shirt waited on a bench inside the main entrance with a couple of shopping bags at her feet, quite a contrast to the doorman in his royal blue and gold uniform. A couple browsed along the window of the closed gift shop, and two teenage boys stood looking up at the long chandelier and discussing something, its engineering, perhaps, or the cracks in the ceiling. None of them showed the slightest interest in us.

Mack hung up and turned toward me, frowning. "I asked for a description," he said. "It was a woman, fat and dark-haired, wearing a denim dress."

"Such as the one April Thorney was wearing when we

saw her, late last night and earlier this morning," I said.

"Exactly."

"Now we know why she was killed."

"Only part of it, J.J.," Mack said. "Only part of it."

Miranda O'Shea, minus Kundala and plus a few clothes, was waiting in the con office when we got there. The old lady with the cat had taken over the big chair, sitting forward eagerly and talking to Miranda about their respective beasts, while the cat dozed on the arm of the chair. Dan Bascombe sat alone at the far end of the table, leafing though a battered magazine with the stunned look of a man who has reached his limit and gone beyond it. My valise was still there.

"When did you last see the snake?" Mack asked, without a hello.

"Just after nine," the girl said. "I got tired of carrying her around—sometimes I think it would be neat if I had a basket with a lid, you know? and maybe lacy-looking sides so I could cart her around on my head"—Mack rolled his eyes and puffed out his cheeks—"well, anyway, she was getting heavy, so a little after nine I took her up and put her in her box."

"What floor is this?" Mack interrupted.

"Sixth." Miranda raised her eyebrows, and Mack nodded. "Then when I went back about ten, just before the costume contest, she was gone," she continued. "Her box, too."

"Did you tell anybody you were putting her to bed?"

"Just whoever I was with when I decided to park her . . . just fans. I don't know their names. Oh, and I rode up in the elevator with Diz and Rita and what's-his-face, Ferraro."

Mack lifted his eyebrows and stared at Miranda. "So we're looking at a time frame of a little less than an hour," he said. "Was the door locked?"

"To the box? It doesn't have a lock."

"To the room."

"Oh. No, of course not."

Mack gave me a see-what-I-mean glance. "So anybody could have walked in and kidnapped the snake. But for what?"

Miranda shrugged and looked toward Dan Bascombe, who was now leafing through the magazine in the other direction.

"More pranks," said the old woman. "Tell Mr. Forrester all about boas, dear. Maybe we can get some ideas."

"Mmm. Well, they're arboreal . . . ."

"Hang it from something," the old woman said, turning to Mack. "Air ducts, maybe? Give the guys playing Killer the shock of their lives." She giggled rustily. "Make 'em pay for their camouflage. Add a touch of real jungle." We all gaped at her. "Go on, honey."

"Let's see. They're strong swimmers."

"That's more likely," Mack said. "Dump the fu—the damn thing in the pool. More visible. Check? More screams. But why did it end up in the salad bar?"

"*In* the salad bar?" Bascombe gasped.

"The restaurant, not the lettuce," I said.

"There you have it," the old woman said, shifting her cat to her shoulder. "Good for you." She shoved herself to her feet with one hand on the arm of the chair and walked out.

"I'm glad you have it," Mack said to me. "Good for you."

"Yeah, good for me," I said. "Soon as I know what I have, I'll let you know."

Bascombe put his hands down, one on each side of the magazine, closed his eyes, and groggily shook his head. "Forrester," he said. "There's something important I keep forgetting to ask you. Do you know where Maureen is?"

"Maureen?" Mack repeated blankly.

168

"Tesla," Bascombe said. "I want to get in touch with her. I don't think she knows about Cass yet."

"Don't tell me you haven't found her yet, Dan!" Miranda said. "Weren't people looking for her all last night?"

"And this morning." Bascombe rubbed his hands over his face. "Nowhere around. Nobody's seen her since after the costume contest. She's not in her room."

"Somebody else's?" Miranda suggested. "But she'd come out by now, wouldn't she? I mean, to eat, or something? That's sixteen hours ago."

"You'd think," Bascombe agreed.

"Crashed somewhere," Mack said.

"She wasn't in the pool last night," Bascombe said. He sounded wider awake and more worried than before. "You know Maureen, she never misses a chance to show off her skin."

Mack's eyebrows jumped and he grinned briefly, but sobered at Bascombe's scowl.

"Maybe after Friday—" Miranda began.

"Hold it," I interrupted. "I just figured out what I got." Everyone stared at me. "The pool was closed for maintenance from nine-thirty to ten-thirty last night," I said. "There were signs up all over the place to stay out, because the chemicals could be harmful to your skin. Let's assume whoever took the snake didn't want to hurt it. Say he picked it up on the spur of the moment, thinking he'd throw a real scare into the skinny-dippers, but he'd forgotten about the pool being closed until he saw the sign. He couldn't put the snake in the pool because of the chemicals, but he was already downstairs with the thing and he had to get rid of it before he was seen. The restaurant is just around the corner from the pool."

"Ah, so," said Mack.

"How he'd get her downstairs without anybody noticing,

I don't know," Miranda objected. "Everybody knows Kundala's mine, and I don't let anybody else handle her without me right there."

"Mmm," I said.

"Look," Mack put in. "If it was Donovan, he's already admitted to the bomb threat and to handing out flyers to the mundanes, and you said he was one of the ones you talked to. He could have hidden her in that robot of his."

"But the robot's not allowed on the first floor," Miranda pointed out. "And the salad bar closes at nine. At nine, Kundala was still with me. I hadn't even put her in her box."

"Yeah, but the salad bar doesn't have a real wall," Mack said, thumping the table with his index finger for each of the last seven words. "Just those planters."

"Why feed her?" Miranda asked. "And what?"

"Keep her quiet," Mack said. "Like you told me downstairs. What he'd give her, I don't know."

"You wouldn't want her quiet in the pool, though," Miranda said. "She'd just climb out and go to sleep."

"Uh-uh. *After* he found out the pool was closed and he had to dump her in a planter, then he had to keep her quiet so she wouldn't get lost. So he fed her."

"Who the hell knows that much about snakes?" Bascombe wondered.

"Anybody who asks me," Miranda said. "Everybody who sees me with her does."

I thought of an objection to my own theory. "She wasn't in one of the wall planters," I said. "She was in one of the inner ones."

"Maybe whoever it was intended to come back and get her when the pool was open again," Mack suggested. "But she sneaked out on him. Would she do that?"

"Maybe," Miranda said doubtfully. "If she thought she was getting away from something that scared her."

170

"Maybe she got a yen for pickled beets," I suggested, and got the glare I deserved from Mack.

"Or maybe," Bascombe said, once again staring at the cobwebs on the ceiling, "she caught her own mouse."

Chapter Fifteen

"WE'RE TAKING A walk," Mack informed me after Miranda headed back to her room. We left Bascombe leafing blindly through the limp magazine, and Mack cop-walked ahead of me down the corridor and across the lounge to the escalator.

"What's up?" I asked. We rode down behind one of the chunkier belly dancers, whose veil floated into Mack's face each time the outside door to the lobby opened.

"You'll see," he said, putting a hand up to ward off the veil and producing a smile as mysterious as any that had ever glimmered behind one.

At the bottom of the escalator we turned left, away from the main entrance. Mack in his invisible uniform still leading the way, we passed the registration desk and the breakfast room, and started along the colonnade that marked the limit of the east wing.

"This is engineers' territory," I commented.

"Check. But only from the second floor up." Mack's lower lip bulged out beneath his bushy mustache. "There ought to be a—yeah, there we go."

He made another left, following an arrow that promised us an exit. We pressed through a swing door into an obviously public hallway painted creamy white and carpeted in gold. A recess in the wall held two pop machines. Opposite them two doors, one labeled with a stylized man and the other with a stylized woman, were blocked open. A cleaning cart stood in the middle of the corridor. Beyond that, parallel blank walls for thirty feet, ending in a door at the other end. Above that door was a lighted exit sign. "Ah-hah," Mack said and sucked in his gut to squeeze past the cart.

The second door opened onto a stairwell almost identical to the one in the north wing, except that it didn't adjoin a service area. Directly ahead and twelve feet away was a third door, this one operated by a pushbar instead of a knob. Large red letters on the door again promised us an exit. Mack pushed the bar.

"There we have it," he announced.

The door opened onto the alley in the wall adjacent to the one where the door had been blocked open beside Cass Grenzman the night before. Mack, holding this door open with both foot and hand, leaned down to look at the lower edge.

"Good paint job," he pronounced. "No chips." He measured the width of the door against his index finger, chewed his mustache for a moment, and retreated into the hall. The door closed gently, clicking a second or two later. Avoiding the pushbar, Mack leaned against the door itself. A tight fit, it didn't even budge.

"Malice aforethought," I said.

Mack glanced at me, one corner of his mouth twitching in a humorless smile, and headed back into the hotel. As we approached the rest rooms, a cleaning woman stumped into the hall and dropped some rags onto her cart.

"Miss?" Mack called.

The woman, gray, drooping, sixtyish, the only color about her the Wellesford Regal gold bandana tightly bound around thin, lank hair looked up with no interest.

"Those blocks you use in the doors," Mack said, nodding at the wooden wedge holding open the door beside her. "Do you leave those here when you're done, or do you take them with you?"

"Leave 'em while the floor dries off," she said, returning

174

her mop to the cart. An overpowering odor of pine oil made me back off.

Mack, on a different scent, rocked on his heels. "How long does that take?"

She shrugged. "Half an hour?"

"Then what happens to the blocks?"

"I come back and kick 'em out and take them up to the second floor and do the rooms there."

"Where are they when nobody's using them?"

"In the cart, in the closet." The woman eyed him. "You police?" she asked.

"Security. Just a couple more questions—like, how often do the bathrooms get cleaned?"

"Once a day, 'less someone complains. That's enough, ain't it?"

"Okay by me," Mack said. He grinned. "Thanks."

The woman nodded without smiling and backed through the swing door into the lobby, dragging her cart.

"Don't look so disappointed," Mack said. "There's other ways to block a door open." He stared hard at the pop machines.

"Thirsty?" I asked.

"Yeah."

He fished some coins out of his pocket and acquired a can of root beer, but instead of popping the top he hustled back down the corridor and opened the outside door. The pop can, lying on its side, held the door open a good two and a half inches. Anyone could grab the edge of the door from outside, haul it open, and be off down the hall.

"Nice," I said.

Mack stared at his handiwork for a moment and shook his head. "No good," he said. "See, you'd have to kick the can out of the way, check? You got no time to stop and reach down for it. If it spins out into the alley, there's a full can of pop laying around to tip somebody off to where you went, check? Last thing you want. People are supposed to think somebody came *in* through the other alley door, a mugger or somebody, who'd take off for the street. Soon as somebody starts thinking you went into the hotel, they're gonna start thinking maybe you came out of it, too, check? So no full cans allowed. If it gets away, you can't just go grab it back. The door might lock you out, and besides, you don't have time."

"Right," I said.

Mack polished the top of the can on his shirttail and popped it open. "So you have to use an empty," he said, starting to drink. "Something nobody would wonder about, tossed into an alley."

"You could get one out of the trash barrel," I pointed out. "If you don't mind getting your hand sticky." Mack nodded, still drinking. "Reminds me of the way you used to go at a can of Blatz," I said.

"Phew." Mack belched. "Filling, that stuff is." He propped the door with the can again with equally good results, except that the can got a little more squashed. The open space was narrower, but still plenty wide enough to yank open the door in a hurry without even stubbing your fingers.

'You want to see malice aforethought," Mack said. "Watch this." He retrieved the can with its two parallel dents, one deeper than the other, took his keys out of his pocket and scratched his initials and the word "dummy" into the side of the can, tossed it into the air, and caught it with a tight smile.

We traipsed through the hall and back up the escalator, Mack with the can in his hand. At the door to conference room D, he spoke briefly to the uniformed man guarding the scene and lounged against the doorjamb as the man went off to confer with Sergeant Ashe.

"It's about last night," Mack said, when the picture-

176

perfect Ashe had waved us in. Mack tossed the can in the air again and caught it. "What you guys should be looking for is a prop for that second door into the alley. I'll bet my nose that's where our killer disappeared to. And there's a whole supply of door props right convenient to that door."

"Oh?" said Ashe.

"A pop machine. What you guys want is a pop can dented just like this one." Mack extended the can with a malicious grin.

"Oh, that," Ashe said. "Yeah, we found it last night. Kicked aside in that corridor runs past the rest rooms."

"Well, look at it this way," I said to Mack, when we were safely clear. "At least you were right."

He looked at me sideways. "They didn't find a pop can in that corridor last night."

"He said—"

"I know what he said. He said he didn't want me messing around on his turf." Mack grinned at me. "Mind games, J.J. Cops play them all the time. He looked at the can, didn't he? He kept it, didn't he?"

"Well, yes."

"Besides, he forgot his geography. He didn't say a word about the stairwell. That's where it would have been kicked to." Mack executed a cheery left toward the con office. "So, our man did just what you'd expect of somebody like him. Picked the can up and chucked it in the barrel next to the pop machines on his way to wherever." His grin became broader. "I'd sure hate to be the sucker has to pick through all that trash."

Sitting demurely at the table in the con office we found the answer to a question: Maureen Tesla, now in jeans and an oversized denim jacket, a little wrinkled. Her yellow hair had gone limp and her face looked drained.

"Mack?" she said, very subdued. She pushed the front

page of the newspaper across the table. "Can you tell me about this? It's true? Cass is dead?"

"Yes." Mack sat sideways on the chair next to her and put one of his big hands on her wrist. "I'm sorry."

She took a deep breath with a tremor at the end. "I'm sorry, too," she said. "I know everybody thinks I'm nothing but a bitch, but I—I'm sorry."

Mack patted her back.

"That's just an act . . . ," Maureen said, trailing off. She spread her oval pink fingernails out in front of her and stared at them. "Mack, I'm one of these people who wants to know everything," she said and inhaled jerkily. "That's how I—how I get rid of ghosts. That's why I came up to talk to you. If I *know*—well, then I don't imagine—what I imagine is always . . . "

"What do you want to know?" Mack asked.

He got a flicker of uncertain smile and a shorter glance. "Well, for instance, what happened." She shrugged. "I mean, the paper says, but it doesn't say, and I keep thinking . . . I hope . . . " Her voice got away from her; she coughed, and with closed eyes asked, "He wasn't shot in the head, was he? In the face?"

"No."

Her whole body drooped. "Oh," she said. "Oh, thank God."

"Where were you?" Mack asked.

"Me?" She blinked at him.

"Last night."

"I . . . " The uncertain smile came back. "How'd you know I wasn't here?"

"We've been looking for you."

"What for?"

"People thought you should know about Cass. Even if you broke up with him, you *are* still on the concom."

"Oh." Maureen blinked several times. "Yeah. I—I met

these guys from the U, and they were kind of bored with the con, and, well, uh, we went to the Uptown for *The Rocky Horror Picture Show* . . . "

I'd never seen *The Rocky Horror Picure Show* myself, but I'd heard from some of the guys I work with that it's one of the world's wilder audience-participation movies. Words to shout, actions to make at certain points in the show. Stuff to smuggle in and throw at the screen, ranging from confetti to raw hot dogs. College kid stuff. The film had been showing at the Uptown for years and was still packing them in.

Maureen winced and buried her face in her hands. "Oh, my God. I was doing all those dumb things and wetting my pants laughing while Cass was getting killed."

She sat for several seconds with her face pressed into her hands, then took a deep breath, straightened without looking at either of us, and reached into her purse for a tissue. She had three or four pocket packs of Kleenex stuffed in there. I wondered if she'd really first learned about Cass in the hotel lobby or somewhere else, somewhere she could let go and cry.

"And then?" Mack said. I hadn't heard his voice that gentle very often. Maureen flashed the smile again.

"I, uh, I went home with a couple of them."

"Were you there all night?"

"Yes." She lifted her chin defiantly. "All night. With both of them."

"What time did you leave the con?" Mack asked.

His lack of instant interest in her overnight activities seemed to throw her. Maureen slumped again. "I don't know. It was during the costume contest. Diz was throwing a fit, and one of the guys said let's get out of here and do something better. We all went up to my room so I could change and we, well, maybe half an hour later we left."

Mack nodded, chewing on his mustache. I calculated. Maureen, if truthful, was in the clear.

"I—we slept real late, and it was a nice day, so I came back just now to collect my stuff and saw the headline on the paper in the box in the lobby, so I bought one and read it right there," Maureen said. "And I came straight up here to see if you could tell me anything—just to, I don't know, keep the nightmares down. I'm glad he wasn't shot in the face." She rubbed at her own forehead. "Have they figured out who—"

"They've arrested Diz Donovan."

"Diz!" Maureen stared at Mack for a moment, and began to giggle and shake her head. "Not Diz. Oh, no. No, no. That's crazy."

"There was an argument—"

"Oh, I heard all about it. But it didn't mean anything. You don't know those two. Diz wouldn't ever, ever kill Cass."

Mack tilted his head, smiled, waited.

"Don't you see?" Maureen leaned forward and seized Mack's hand, gazing into his eyes like the Maureen of Friday night. "Diz wouldn't want Cass dead," she said, her voice low and intense. "Terrified, maybe, but never dead. He'd want to be able to work on him, you know? Like with these pranks he's been playing on the con."

"Itching powder instead of a gun." Mack extracted his hand and leaned back.

"Yes, exactly." Maureen's forehead wrinkled. She caught her lower lip under her teeth. "They've got the wrong man," she said. "Mack, help me. I want to find out who really did it."

"Do you?" he asked. "Why?"

"Oh, please. Cass, he's a jerk sometimes, but I love him. I was just being bitchy yesterday. Sooner or later we'd have gotten back together." She sniffled. "We always did before."

"How do you think I can help?" Mack asked, tipping his chair back, arms behind his head.

180

"Tell me everything you know."

"Deal, if you'll answer a couple of questions first."

"Okay," Maureen said warily. One of the headsets lying on the table blurted a word. Mack reached out and turned it off.

"How did you know Diz was playing the pranks?" Mack asked.

"I saw him."

Mack raised his eyebrows but said nothing. Five seconds went by. *Ask her, ask her,* I wanted to shout.

"Friday afternoon," she said finally. "I'm sorry about needling you, out on the street that night. That was Cass's idea. I'd told him about Diz." She showed her teeth, a glimpse of ferocity she quickly hid. "I wish I hadn't."

"What did you see?"

"Him taking a couple of those fake bombs out of the robot in the hall on the sixth floor. He was really funny about it, looked all around a couple of times before he opened the thing up. I'd come up the stairs from the fifth and had just opened the door maybe so wide"—she held her hands three inches apart—"and I saw him. He didn't see me, so I just hung back and watched."

Mack nodded. *Why come up the stairs?* I wondered.

"He had a couple of brown paper packages in his hands when he turned, and he was wearing those white cotton gloves he puts on when he eats, so I wondered if he had some kind of food. But then he stuffed the packages inside his shirt and got onto the elevator. So I thought it couldn't be food."

She looked carefully into Mack's face, and he nodded again.

"So I went and looked into the robot after he left. There were a few more little packages in there, stuck up with masking tape, with telephone wire coming out. I opened one and saw it was only candles, so I wrapped it back up and put it back. Then when the cops came around and said there were bombs, I knew right away what he'd been doing."

She wasn't scared, I thought. That was what had bothered me Friday, beyond the teasing. She wasn't scared, nor was Cass. And Diz had wanted to finish his grape juice.

"Is that all?" Maureen asked, after Mack had gazed at her, poker-faced, for a few more seconds.

"And you didn't say anything?" Mack asked. "Warn Dan about what was happening?"

"Why should I?" She smoothed the damp Kleenex over her fingers. "He was acting strange, but Diz is Diz. He's always a little on the weird side. And like I said, I didn't really put it together until they emptied the hotel. I guess I—I was a little high, I guess I didn't really think about it. And then, well, he's kind of a friend. I mean, I've known him a long time. And it didn't seem like any real damage was done. I mean, the cops had a lot of trouble, sure, but nobody . . . I didn't want to get him in bad trouble. Poor Diz."

"You didn't happen to see him with the snake, did you?" Mack asked.

"Snake?"

"Belongs to Miranda O'Shea. It went missing last night, but she's got it back now."

"Oh. Kundala." She shook her head. "Sorry."

"Or anything else? Making a phone call, turning out lights, renting X-rated videotapes?"

"Renting porno flicks? Diz?"

"Somebody did, and put them in with the tapes the con was showing. They were found before any damage was done. I don't *know* that it was Diz, but it makes things simpler if it was."

Maureen let slip a wicked little smile. "I wish I'd been there to see him ask for them," she said. She sighed. "But I wasn't."

182

"How long have you been going with Cass Grenzman?" Mack asked.

"Four years, off and on." She pressed the tissue to her nose.

"You must know him pretty well then. Could he have done some of the tricks? Knowing the bomb scare was a trick, maybe figured to give the con, or maybe just Diz, more trouble? Stuffed the ovens with tablecloths and opened the refrigerators, say?"

"If it happened after they threw him out of the pool, yeah, he could've," Maureen said. "It'd be like him to. But he didn't say. I guess I didn't really give him a chance—not that he would've said anything if I had."

Mack chewed his mustache for a few seconds and shrugged. "Okay, ask your questions," he said.

She got down to business instantly. "Where was he shot?"

"Through the heart. Twice."

Maureen clutched at her shirt. "No, I mean *where*—location."

"Bottom of the stairwell next to the service area. He was playing Killer with a bunch of guys in camouflage."

"And one of them had a real gun with a piece of green tape on it." Maureen nodded. The tip of her tongue slipped out between compressed lips. "Good place. I can think of six ways into it." She cast a glance at Mack to see if he was listening. "First floor door, stairs down, stairs up, alley, there's a real door and some kind of garage doors, service elevator, kitchen. Oh, and there's another door, employees only, but that's locked. There's usually some laundry carts left in the service area you can use for cover. Cass must have been stalking somebody."

"You know a lot about it," Mack remarked.

"Oh, I play, too," she said. "I did Friday, before I found out about the pool thing. Cass always got a real turn-on out of me playing." She paused, but got no reaction. "Which way was he facing?"

"Toward the first floor door," Mack said grudgingly.

"Then somebody came through that door?"

"Possibly."

Maureen sat thinking this over. "What time?" she asked.

"Oh, eleven-thirtyish."

Eleven-forty-seven, to be precise.

Maureen's face wrinkled again. She shook her head. "At least I wasn't throwing rice yet," she said.

"Come again?"

"*Rocky Horror*. There's a wedding in the movie and you throw rice at the screen. I'm glad his face wasn't marked."

"His face was marked," I said. Mack closed his eyes, eyebrows raised, and shrugged.

She turned on Mack. "You lied," she said, fists tight. "I asked you was he shot in the face and you said no, his heart."

"Not shot, marked," Mack said. "There was a streak of blood right across his upper lip and running down on one side, like this." He demonstrated on his own face.

"Almost as if somebody drew a mustache," Maureen said slowly. "Oh, God! You don't think, I mean, would a killer stop to draw a mustache on him? That's sick."

"He wouldn't have had time. Besides, we know Cass drew it himself," Mack said. "There was blood on the first two fingers of his right hand."

"His right hand?" Maureen said. Her delicate brows arched. "Are you sure?"

"Absolutely."

"Then Cass didn't draw it," she said confidently. "No way. Cass was lefthanded."

184

Chapter Sixteen

"THERE'S SOMETHING ELSE you should know," Mack said, rousing Maureen from deep thought. "Something that wasn't in the paper. April Thorney's dead."

"April?" The color drained from Maureen's face and flooded back. "April's dead, too?"

Mack nodded.

"Shot?"

"No." Mack sighed. "You remember the knife that was stolen yesterday? She was stabbed."

Maureen's hands moved to her chest and crossed protectively between her breasts.

"In the throat," Mack said.

Her hands crept slowly up to her throat, still crossed, and she caressed the angle of her jaw on both sides. "When?" she whispered.

"Last night. I think she must have known, or known something that would let her figure out, who killed Cass."

"I get you." Maureen stared at the wall for a moment, then got to her feet. Fists shoved into her narrow jacket pockets, the sleeves rucked up halfway to her elbows against the pocket flaps, she went to the door, stared into the corridor for a moment, and turned.

"Go get him, Mack," she said.

"Get who?"

She half-smiled, stepped through the door without speaking, and closed it gently behind her.

"Whom," Mack corrected himself bleakly. He gave his face a thorough rub and exhaled. "What the hell are we doing, J.J.?" he asked. "Where's our plain common sense?"

"Doing? Something wrong with what we're doing?"

"Having kids in this day and age." He slammed his hand against the table. "At least you've only got one. I've got three, and one of them's a girl."

"What are you talking about?"

He got up and opened the door Maureen had just shut. "Her," he said, vehement. "Kids like her. Our kids, yours, mine, ten, fifteen years from now."

"Maureen? Well, she's a little, uh . . . " I couldn't find a word that seemed to suit the woman.

"A little 'uh.'" He plunked into the armchair. "Check. How much you think that habit costs a day? Where does the money come from, the moon?"

"I missed that," I said.

"Where are your *eyes*, man?" Mack sat back, forehead in wrinkles. "When I think of my Mary Ellen, nine years old . . . she's just a little girl. And hell, kids a year or two older than she is get picked up with their pockets full of crack. And here I might just as well be stuffing it in. Where's my head?" He shook his head, showing no sign he'd noticed its presence. "Remember, J.J.? You and me, all we were up to at that age was walking around after Mass, trying to find some girl with patent-leather shoes. And then I see a kid like Maureen—"

"—who must be almost an entire decade younger than you," I said. "Come off it, Mack. You weren't exactly a saint in high school yourself."

"Yeah, but I wasn't a father, then," Mack said, letting the front legs of his chair hit the floor. "I don't think."

One of the twins walked in, laid a headset on the table, and sat down. "When?" she asked with a grin, resting her elbows on the table and lacing her fingers under her chin. "And why not?"

186

"Never mind," Mack said. He nodded at the headset. "Where'd you find that?"

"Fell out from under Miranda O'Shea's mattress when she pulled a sheet off the bed to wrap up her snake. I met her in the elevator coming down, and the snake wasn't real happy in the sheet, so she gave the radio to me to bring in."

Mack began stroking his mustache with his index finger.

"It is one of ours, isn't it?" the twin asked. "It looks the same. Same brand and everything."

"If it wasn't, it is now," Mack said. He stopped stroking his mustache and frowned into space. "Marie . . ."

Marie, or Michelle being polite, waited.

"Marie, do you remember how many headsets were on the table when you picked one up to keep track of that game?"

"Sorry."

"Try."

She closed her eyes for several seconds. "Three?" she asked, after a long sigh.

"Wait." Mack, still frowning, started counting slowly on his fingers. "Should have been four," he said. "Shouldn't there?"

"Who was on?" Marie asked.

"You and your sister, and Dan, and one of my old ladies. And I think Grenzman had borrowed one. You left yours at the pool. Three were out with concom members. That's eight. Eight from twelve is four."

"What about Wade?"

"Yates was on, too, but he was in the office by then." He turned to me. "Did Yates have a headset with him when he showed up downstairs?" he asked.

"Sure. I remember him holding it up when Bascombe asked why he'd taken so long."

"But he hadn't taken that long," Mack said, sitting forward. "He showed up right after Bascombe. Check?" I wonder . . . why was Bascombe complaining?"

"Might have seemed like a long time to him. Working in an elementary school, he's probably not used to bodies lying around just any old where," I said. "Not full-grown ones, anyway," but sarcasm was lost on Mack.

"What—," Marie began.

"Remember how he reacted when I told him Donovan was the prankster?" Mack interrupted. "He said it had to be Grenzman, check? And he turned a funny color." He looked away. "Like he might if he'd taken care of, uh, the wrong problem."

"Dan couldn't have killed Cass," Marie said. "He was with us. At the pool."

"All the time?"

"Well, he was at one end, and Michelle was in the middle, and I was at the far end. We divided it up."

"Was he where you could see him?"

"Of course he was. How far out of sight of the pool can you get? There's only those few tables."

"What about the lights? How much light was there?"

"Little ones on the tables, and the pool lit up, and a spot on each ladder. The other ceiling lights on low. You know how they set it up."

Mack wriggled slightly, like a cat getting ready to pounce. "So if Bascombe had been missing for a few minutes, you wouldn't have noticed."

"I . . . " Marie swallowed. "Well, maybe not. Not if I happened to be talking to somebody, I guess. I wasn't supposed to be keeping an eye on Dan, of all people."

"No, no. 'Course not," Mack said. He gripped his hands over his head, scowling so deeply that the girl drew back. "'Course not," he said under his breath. "It had to be all set up in advance. Check?" he said to me. "The doors, I mean. Question is, how long could he leave it that way? We *all* had headsets, all of us, the cops, too, the rent-a-cops were on our frequency! So he'd know when Grenzman was heading for the stairs. And he'd know who else was close by and where they'd called in from. He'd know if the open doors had been discovered. Then he'd need what, three minutes, four? Shit," Mack added, in admiration.

"Mack?" said the twin, as if he'd taken leave of his senses.

"Was he out of breath?" Mack demanded, leaning forward again. "Did you notice if he was panting?"

"Mack, I just told you," the girl protested. She sounded bewildered. "It was all okay, everything was normal. I don't know what you're thinking he could have done, but Dan was at the pool. I'm sure of it."

"How can you be sure of it if you didn't see him?"

"Well—I saw him every time I looked!"

"Every time you looked," Mack said, with slow emphasis. "And how often was that?"

She shrugged. "Every few minutes."

"That's all he needed," Mack declared, triumphant. "A few minutes. Just three or four fucking minutes!"

"When did he set it up?" I asked.

"Any time! He could have run out a couple of times before without anybody seeing. Two minutes here, two minutes there."

I reached for the phone.

"What are you doing?" Mack asked.

"Calling Karen," I said.

"What for?"

"'I want to talk to her."

Mack got up and started for the door.

"Hold on, don't go till I talk to her," I said.

He leaned against the jamb, folded his arms, and narrowed his eyes. The twin stared at me.

By the tenth ring, I was ready to hang up, but Karen picked up the receiver and said a breathless, "Jam'sons."

"Karen, I need the answer to a question . . . yes, before I get home," I said when she started to sputter. "Can you tell me who was at that workshop yesterday? The one where people read what they'd written?" Mack frowned, and the twin straightened and gazed past him.

"Just a minute, I'll check my notebook," Karen said. "I did a couple of character sketches."

She came back to the phone a minute later. "Yes, I've got almost a whole list," she reported.

"First, who was the one with the stories in mailers?"

She read off a name and I wrote it down. The twin glanced quickly at me and down at her lap. Mack's hands came down and rested on his hips.

"Okay, who else was there?"

Only a dozen people had come, including herself. She'd amused herself by writing down the badge names and trying to guess what the real ones might be, and as the people introduced themselves she'd added the real ones to chasten herself.

"Dan Bascombe?"

"No. Helen was. His wife. And Sue Evers was there, she's that woman with the long red hair who came into your lecture after the lights went out, with that gorgeous blue velvet dress. Remember? And Maureen Tesla, but she didn't read anything. In fact, she left before we really got started. Wade Yates, he's pretty good, and someone named Simon Calvin Aloysius Turnipseed who called himself Sicat, I kid you not . . . "

I let her finish, but I'd heard what I wanted. I thanked her and hung up. Mack still leaned against the door; and Marie the Vulcan had folded her arms to watch me with a blank, suspicious gaze that gave me the willies. I cleared my throat.

"What time did Yates relieve you at the pool, Marie?" I asked.

"Friday, you mean? That was Michelle on duty Friday."

"No. Saturday. Last night."

Mack straightened and came to the table, hulked over me for a moment, and abruptly sat.

Marie looked puzzled. "He didn't relieve us at all. Was he supposed to?"

"Not at all?" Mack said.

"No. Dan and Michelle and I were down there when you called Dan on the headset. He told Michelle he was leaving, and we divided the pool in half."

"He wasn't at the pool then? Yates?"

"Not that I saw. He could have been sitting at one of the back tables, I guess, I wasn't really watching what was going on there." She smiled briefly. "I figured if nobody was yelling, what they did was their business."

"He wasn't on duty at the pool?"

"No! Are you listening? Your call came in, and Dan went rushing off, and Michelle and I just kept on going. I heard Dan call for Wade, but since it wasn't for me I didn't pay much attention, and then nothing until you called me up to the con office to monitor Cass's game. And you know where Wade was then, he was in the office with us."

"Yeah," Mack said, almost choking on the word.

"Can I go? Michelle's waiting, and we've got some good-byes to say and a long bus ride."

"Sure," Mack said, dispiritedly. "Thanks for everything."

"Oh, sure. It was kind of fun," Marie said. "Except for last night."

Mack shut the office door and leaned against it. "Bascombe," he said. "Not Yates."

"Why not?"

"Because, J.J., I have observed that Bascombe is *also* left-handed. Yates isn't. You're facing me. Which hand is on the same side as my right?"

"My left," I said. "But we already agreed that there wasn't time for the murderer to draw that mustache."

"You still think Grenzman did it himself? For what?"

"To tell us who had shot him," I said. "Isn't that the usual idea? Deathbed accusations?"

"What the hell would he think a mustache would tell us?" Mack demanded, coming to the table to lean over it and shout at me. "Everybody in the whole case has a mustache, except you and the snake! Including Bascombe."

"Not *a* mustache. *That* mustache. The one that has a long tail on each side, and whose owner has a habit of tugging always and only at the tail on the right!"

Mack's lower lip came up tight. He squinted at me. I stood up. He may be bigger, but I'm still quicker.

"Whose owner was at a fantasy-writing workshop yesterday afternoon that was also attended by a would-be writer who keeps his work protected in padded mailers," I continued, side-stepping my chair. "Ten by fourteens, Mack. Big enough to mail other things than manuscripts."

"Where'd you hear that?"

"Karen. She told me about it as a joke at dinner last night, but I didn't make the connection until a few minutes ago."

"Hell," Mack said. "Hell." He sagged to sit on the table. "Ah, but that won't go," he said, whirling to point at me. "Anybody who emptied that mailbox would feel the shape of the gun through the mailer, check?"

"Not if it had toilet paper stuffed around it."

He shrugged and sighed.

"Mack, Yates had a headset, too. He had every opportunity Bascombe did. He could have walked right up"—inspiration, in the form of a near-vision, seized me—"with the gun under that Jedi warrior costume of his, asked to borrow the headset—"

"Why didn't he use his own?"

"The idea was to get Grenzman's away from him, remember?"

"So why didn't Grenzman tell him to go fly? He should have had a headset of his own."

"Don't you get it? Yates wasn't on duty yet. He didn't even have to say so, not with that costume on. He just had to say he'd seen something or somebody had told him about something, like the snake in the laundry we were talking about, and ask to borrow it. Then out comes the gun—" Mack began shaking his head. I plunged on. "It fits, Mack, it all fits! The costume comes off in the men's room. He rolls the gun up in it and shoves the bundle somewhere. Then he comes running—"

"How does he know to come running?"

"He's got Grenzman's headset. Or one of them, anyway, they all look alike. That's why one was missing last night. He couldn't show up with two. He had to ditch one."

"J.J.," Mack said. "You've got no idea what a straight arrow Yates is. I just can't see this. Okay, opportunity, I grant you, and he's fast on his feet up here"—Mack tapped his skull—"as well as otherwise. But what about motive?"

"You got me there," I said.

"Little squabbles, that's all I ever saw. Now Bascombe, he's got the motive—"

"Motive," I said. "What motive?"

"Money! Money! You told me yourself this morning, money!" Mack jumped up and walked around the table. I backed off. "Believe me, J.J., after scraping the bottom of my savings account to post bond for my license, if there's one motive I know all about, it's money. And Bascombe's just as smart as the rest of them. No more out of shape, either. He was just around the corner—"

"Damn it, Mack, they can't *both* have been at the pool!"

He frowned. "It doesn't seem as if they can both not have been, either. Or could they? Bascombe didn't say anything about Yates not being there . . . oh, of course! He wasn't there himself, so he couldn't be sure whether Yates had reported yet or not."

"The guy would have to have jet-assisted roller skates to

whizz around the way you—"

"So would Yates! So would Yates! He'd only just called in three minutes before—"

"—and checked your position."

"And he'd have to get from, where was it, the con suite down to the pool—"

"—where he said he already was."

"Just got there, and—"

The telephone beside my elbow rang. I picked it up and said, "Con office."

"Mack?" said a small, breathless voice. "Marie. There's trouble up here, room five-twelve." She hung up.

"Trouble upstairs," I told Mack. "Room five-twelve."

"That's Yates's room." He jerked his head at the door. "Let's go."

Chapter Seventeen

MACK THUMBED THE elevator button. "Who was that on the phone?" he asked.

"Marie. She sounded scared."

"Sheesh, why didn't you say so?" he asked, turning away. "I'd have taken the stairs."

The elevator doors opened. Mack reversed his direction midstride and we stepped in, Mack pushing the fifth floor button and the close door button with finger and thumb of the same big hand. For once, the elevator rose the three floors we wanted without interruption.

"What's up?" Mack asked, met at the opening doors by both twins.

"Wade's got a knife on Maureen," one of them said.

Mack took a quick step in the direction of room 512. "Easy, easy," the other twin said. She put both hands against his chest and pushed him back. "He's threatening to kill her if anybody comes near the room."

I noticed, now, a cluster of half a dozen frightened-looking fans gathered at the far end of the corridor, none of them speaking. Ferraro was the only one I recognized among them. He raised his chin at me, mouth open to breathe, but said nothing. The rest stared past us at the opposite end of the corridor.

The door of 512 stood open. Maureen stepped carefully through it. Her fists were deep in the pockets of the denim coat, so tense I was sure she had been told to keep them there. Yates had a fistful of her hair in his left hand, and her head was pulled back so far I wondered how she kept

195

her balance. With his right hand Yates held a knife to her throat. He sidestepped to keep Maureen between himself and us, and backed slowly toward the service stairs, Maureen faltering after him.

"Wade," Mack said. He sounded surprised, concerned—the tone he might take with a child about to do something unexpected and dangerous.

"A warning, Mack," Yates said. "Maureen and I are going down these stairs. If I hear anyone enter the stairwell from any level, I will use this knife. Is that clear?"

In his turn, he sounded as if he had just given a homework assignment to a class of fifth-graders. I couldn't believe he meant a threat. But the knife point hovered close to Maureen's throat without a tremor.

"Wade, think it over," Mack pleaded.

That brought a small smile. "I have thought it over," Yates said. "That's the whole problem, too much thinking it over." Maureen's wide stare did not change. Her face was pale, with two spots of color on her cheeks, and her teeth chattered.

"Wade—"

"You heard me," Yates stated. He leaned against the door with its contradictory *Exit* and *Employees Only* signs. It opened.

He backed through, pulling Maureen after him. "Slower," she gasped. "Wade, please, I can't walk like this." His left hand only tightened in her hair. Both were on the landing now. Yates gave the door a kick to swing it wider and jerked the blond through, sidling behind the door for cover as it closed.

"Oh, jeez, oh," Mack breathed. He ran for the open door of room 512, pausing as he entered to call to the knot of fans, "Don't anybody use the elevator, check?"

The twins and I followed. When I got to the room, Mack had the phone in his hand and had just finished dialing.

"Answer," he said impatiently. "Where the hell's the clerk?"

"Mack?" one of the twins said.

"You," he said, dialing again. "Take the left-hand elevator up two floors. Listen against the service door. Whatever you do, don't open it! Just see if you can figure out if he's taking her up. If you hear them coming, for God's sake get out of the way. When you figure out which way they're going, report."

"How?"

"Oh, crap, the one time we really need the stupid damn headsets and we don't have them. Get down to the cops in conference room D as fast as you can and report to them. Don't tie up both elevators." He shook the telephone receiver as the twin whirled and disappeared. "Where the hell's room service when you need it?" he demanded. "You," he said to the other twin. "Get downstairs fast and tell those cops what's happening."

Ferraro showed up at the door and said, "I brought an elevator down. Marie's using it. Anything else I can do?"

"Just a sec," Mack said, dialing. "Hey!" he said into the phone. "Get me the police in conference room D. It doesn't have a phone? Well, get me some kind of line to them. It's an emergency! What? Oh, Christ! Call 911. Tell them to go to the conference room. D! D! D! And on no account use the service stairs!"

He almost threw the phone into its cradle. "She thinks they've left. Come on," he said, collecting me and Ferraro.

We sprinted for the elevators. Mack glanced up at the floor indicators and pounded on the call button. "You'll listen at the service door on the third floor," he told Ferraro. "You heard what I said to Michelle?"

"No."

Mack repeated his instructions, staring at the floor indicator. "Come on, come *on*," he urged the elevator. "J.J., you come with me. First floor, I guess. Yeah."

"What if the cops have left?" Ferraro asked.

"Wait there. Tell them what's going down. Ah! Finally!"

We got into the car, and Mack punched the buttons for the third and first floors as if he wanted to put them clean through the wall.

At the third floor Ferraro was out of the car almost before the doors could open, and Mack punched at the door closer. "She's too smart for her britches," he said. "Why couldn't she leave it to the pros?"

"Who?"

"Maureen!" His fists were clenched.

The doors opened on the first floor and we nearly bowled over an elderly man waiting patiently for the elevator as we dashed out. Mack sprinted past the registration desk, where there was no clerk, and into the colonnade between the core and the north wings. He wanted the other stairs, I saw.

"Mack," I panted. "You'll get her stabbed."

"Not this one," he said.

He bashed though the swing door into the long, fortunately empty corridor and took the length of it in about six leaps. At the door, he stopped.

"Listen," he said, panting. "We're going downstairs. Quiet. Like spiders. I think he's going to try to get out through the garage. I'll try to talk to him there. But we've got to be *quiet* going down."

"I got you," I said.

We went almost silently into the stairwell. Mack paused to listen. Nothing. He led the way down the stairs into the basement level, where the brightly lit, glass-walled airlock opened onto the dim parking garage. We were still breathing heavily, mouths open to mask the sound. I could already taste stale exhaust. Mack eased open the door, and we stepped into the garage. The latch snicked behind us.

Mack closed his eyes and his lips moved, three or four words. The airlock of the other stairs was only yards away, across a few parked cars.

Mack pointed. We moved away from the bright light of the glassed enclosure into the shadow of a concrete pillar. Street noise came though the open ramp of the garage and echoed from the concrete walls. Mack started to speak, and was drowned in the roar of an accelerating bus. He shook his head.

Legs descended the stairs into the bright, glass cage across the way—Maureen's. Close behind, Wade's. He still had her hair in his fist. The hand with the knife rested on her right shoulder, the blade held close beside her eye. She felt for each step before shifting her weight, hands still tense in her jacket pockets. They must have come down the whole six flights that way.

"Poor kid," I murmured.

"Hss," Mack said, shoving me down behind a car. He grabbed my head and pulled my ear close to his mouth. "We'll let him get ahead," he breathed. "I'll sneak after him. When I'm close, make some kind of noise. You'd better be nearer the ramp. Go."

I took a moment to scout my route, not happy with Mack's plan but with nothing better to offer. There weren't as many cars as I'd have liked. People had been leaving the con early. What if somebody came down to claim his car while Wade still had Maureen in the garage?

Worry about that if it happens, I told myself.

The door of the other airlock opened. A moment later it closed again, surely much louder than our own had been. "Wade, please," Maureen said. "Just run for it. I promise—"

Under cover of her voice Mack had moved through shadow and gained a parking row closer to the two. I moved myself, shaking, out of the safety of the pillar's shadow. A brand-new Buick sheltered me now. I hoped I'd made as little sound as Mack had.

"You're coming with me," Wade told Maureen.

"Wade, you're crazy, we can't go through the street this way!"

Mack slipped closer. Or I assumed so. He wasn't where he had been, but I couldn't see him. I aimed for shadow behind another pillar, crawled into it and stood up.

"You'll walk beside me," Wade said. "I still have your key."

"Wade . . . "

They were starting up the ramp. I stretched, looking for Mack, and couldn't see him. I took a step sideways.

Something I hadn't seen in the shadow toppled over with an echoing thump. My stomach lurched. Wade pulled Maureen's head back, and lowered the knife. "Who's there?" he yelled.

I leaned against the pillar, breathing through my mouth, sure my heartbeat was echoing as loudly as whatever I'd knocked over. I glanced down and saw a large wooden box with slatted sides and bottom and a hardware cloth inset in its top. Kundala's cage.

Among the street noises I heard a siren.

"Who is that?" Yates demanded.

My knees felt weak. I slid slowly down the pillar to squat against it.

"Wade," Mack said.

"Mack! Where—? There's two of you, who's—?"

"Wade," Maureen whimpered. "That hurts."

The siren died in a throaty purr. A squad car pulled up to the ramp exit and blocked it off. The red light reflected into the garage, bouncing off concrete and chrome, lighting Maureen's face like flashes of blood. Peering between cars, I still couldn't see Mack. The squad car door slammed.

200

"No!" Maureen screamed. "Don't come any closer!"

"Put the knife down, Wade," Mack said. He had the same firm, no-nonsense tone Yates had used on the fifth floor. It made me shake my head.

"Get out of here, Mack," Yates said. "Maureen, we're going back into the hotel."

"I can't," she wailed.

"Put the knife down," Mack said. "This isn't what you wanted."

"What would you know about what I want?"

"No," Maureen said shakily. "Wade, he's right. It's not what you wanted. Remember yesterday?"

"Yesterday was much too long ago," Yates said.

Someone in a blue uniform crouched behind the outermost car in the garage. I wasn't sure how he'd got there. His hand was on the butt of the gun in his holster.

"Yesterday was only yesterday," Mack said. "It's gone wrong, hasn't it? But you don't have to make it worse."

"Please, Wade," Maureen said. "I promise, I'll never do another line in my life."

The man in the blue uniform was no longer behind the outermost car. I couldn't spot him, or Mack.

"It's too late for that," Yates said.

"Not too late," Mack said. "Never too late. Please, Wade. Put the knife down."

I heard a shoe scrape on concrete halfway down the ramp. "Is that Jamison?" Yates asked. "Or a cop?"

I sat down on Kundala's box.

"Three of you now," Yates said. "Must be a cop. I'll kill her, you hear?" he shouted. "I've got a knife on her and I know how to use it."

"Won't do any good," Mack said. "Just someone else on your conscience. You didn't want to kill April, did you?"

"April—" Yates said. His voice had gone high.

"All she did was listen to you. Isn't that it?" Mack said.

"All she did was be a friend, buy a few stamps."

"Oh, God," Yates said. "You know about that? You know about that?"

"Drop it!" said a new voice.

"Wade, no!" Maureen screamed.

I heard a grunt of surprise and pain, and shivered. Something, someone, fell. I dropped my head into my hands.

"Get an ambulance," Mack snapped.

The cop dashed up the ramp and launched his upper body through the open window of his car. A minute later he dragged himself out and ran back down the ramp. Two other uniformed men followed. Somebody opened the door of one of the airlocks.

"What's going on?" a woman asked.

"Emergency," Mack said. "Go back upstairs."

"But my car—"

"Not now. Ten minutes," said the first cop.

Someone was sobbing. The sound echoed off the concrete walls, ghostly, desolate, like something out of an Irish folktale. The simile pleased me. I wondered if Karen would want it for her notebook. Probably not.

"J.J., where the hell are you?" Mack called.

"Here."

"Well, get over here."

The first cop ran back up the ramp to move his car as the siren of an ambulance drew closer. "He's not going to make it," Mack said, when I'd dragged myself up and walked over.

Yates lay on his side on the concrete, knees pulled up, scarcely breathing. The knife protruded from his chest, just below the ribs; the hilt angled downward. *He must have hit his heart*, I thought. Hunkered beside him, Maureen pressed her face into her hands and tightened herself into a fetal ball.

"My own knife," she moaned. "My own knife. It's my

knife." She began sobbing again. I crouched beside her and put my hand on her back, but she shrugged it away.

"Later," Mack said. I didn't plan to be around later.

"What in hell is going on?" asked the woman, who had not gone back up the stairs. One of the cops took her by the elbow and walked her away. She stared over her shoulder at us as she went.

The ambulance pulled up. Doors slammed. A pair of paramedics raced down the ramp, and the ambulance backed slowly after them as they examined Yates.

"I want to go with him," Maureen said.

"Who's she?" one of the cops asked Mack.

"No relation," Mack said. "You'll want to talk to her."

"I think you'd better come with me, then, Miss—?"

"Tesla," Mack supplied.

"You're Forrester, right?" the cop said. "Sergeant Ashe is upstairs in room D. He wants to talk to you."

"I bet he does," Mack sighed. "Let's go, J.J. Nothing we can do here."

I followed him back up the stairs. Neither of us had anything to say.

As he talked to Mack, and my old friend with the bushy eyebrows talked to me. When he was done, I sat on one of the benches of the central lounge to wait for Ashe to be finished with Mack. Across the way, the closing program of the con was being held. Enough people had stayed to make the ceremony noisy, though the sound lacked the contagious ebullience I'd heard less than forty-eight hours before.

Mack joined me as people started streaming out of the room where the ceremonies had been held. He watched them for a moment. Few were in costume, and while they chattered loudly enough, the mood was subdued.

"Take me a few minutes to pack up here," Mack said.

"I'm going to go call Joy right now." He glanced at me, unsmiling. "Jeez, do I want to go home. I can hardly remember what it looks like."

Chapter Eighteen

THE WHOLE HOUSE smelled tantalizingly of roast turkey. Even over the game on TV in the family room, I could hear it crackling and sizzling in the oven. My mouth watered.

Karen and Joy bustled in the kitchen, putting the final touches on Thanksgiving dinner. Our four kids had set the table an hour ago. Mack's super-salad waited in the refrigerator for a final toss with his secret dressing—out of a Wishbone bottle—and Joy's pumpkin and mince pies stood at the back of the counter looking ready to be photographed for a magazine. Mack and I had decided to sneak in a little football watching before the feast.

I'd had the foresight to lock up all the computer disks that held any programs or data I wanted to keep, and over the announcer's comments on the football game I could hear the kids downstairs arguing over the computer games I'd left out. Joey was showing off, since he was the one who knew the peculiarities of my system; Mack's son Mickey was trying to trade on being twice Joey's age. Between them, I figured I'd be called down to the basement to rescue something any minute.

Mack turned the glass of beer in his hand, looking through it at the television. "Thanks for inviting us," he said abruptly.

"Hey, Thanksgiving's late this year," I said. "Karen's folks are in Florida and mine don't want to take a chance on getting stuck in the snow between here and home. You don't expect us to have a dinner for three on turkey day, do you? Too quiet."

"Quiet this is not," Mack agreed. Downstairs, Mary Ellen out-shouted all three boys.

On the television, the announcer casually mentioned something about some ball player who'd finished a course of treatment for drug abuse and was back on the field.

Mack nodded at the screen. "Reminds me. Did you ever figure out all of that business last month?" he asked.

"At the con? No. I saw in the paper that Donovan was being charged with a few things for that bomb scare, but that's all."

"I've spent a lot of time on the phone, lately. And I've been talking to my friend Al," Mack said. "I think I've got it put together now."

"Yeah?"

He sighed. "We were missing one very important piece of info, J.J. That Friday wasn't the first time Cass Grenzman and Maureen Tesla had broken up. In fact, for about five months last spring, she was dating Wade Yates."

"Ah-huh," I said.

Somebody on the TV screen fumbled the ball.

"Butterfingers," Mack commented.

"That much I can figure out for myself," I said.

"Oh, yeah. Well. I told you what a straight arrow Yates is—was."

His lower lip pushed upward, and his mustache splayed out. For a minute or two, I thought he'd finished. But he was only thinking.

"He could stand to see Maureen go back to Cass, though he wasn't happy about it," Mack continued. "He knew she'd dated him before, and Wade's a stoic type. I guess he thought he was just being realistic. Still, when she broke up with Cass after the business at the pool—"

"I never did know what that was, exactly," I said.

"Oh, he was just wandering around grabbing at people's bodies. They didn't like it."

206

"Who would?"

Mack shrugged. "Anyway, Wade got hopeful. He discussed the matter with April Thorney, who encouraged him to go talk to Maureen, which was when he learned that Cass had her hooked on cocaine. She'd been clean when she was going with Wade. She's in treatment now, by the way. She could pick up some dope at the con, but when the con ended, that was it. Without Grenzman, she'd have to find her own source. No problem, I guess, but she'd have to pay cash. And where was the cash going to come from? By Saturday noon she was crazy to get back with Grenzman and had a few words to say to Wade about himself. Loudly. 'Dull, dull, dull, dull and boring' was the quote I heard."

"Where did Grenzman get the stuff?" I asked.

Mack squeezed his eyes shut. "There's where I really guessed wrong. I should have paid more attention to what he said about you—that you were nothing to worry about. He was selling it."

"At the con?"

"Some. Crack, mostly. This I did not discuss with Al."

I nodded. "I bet you didn't. Yates found out?"

"I think so."

"And he decided to get rid of a bad influence," I said.

I remembered the old woman with the cat: vengeance is transitive. But is it transitive, if the person doesn't ask to be avenged? Or is it still just for oneself, plain and simple?

"I guess you could put it that way," Mack agreed. "Anyway, he decided to get rid of Cass as fast as he could, and do it at the con because he figured there'd be safety in numbers. First he stole the knife because he figured no one could trace it to him. Then he went to that workshop, saw the mailers, and came up with what he thought was a better plan, pretty much what we figured out the next day. The gun was his own. He home and picked it up Saturday evening. He lived about a ten minute walk away. He was kind enough to notify me that he was going out of the hotel for dinner and wouldn't be available for security detail."

"Wait, hold on. He saw the mailers and came up with the plan? I don't get you."

"His own gun, check? Perfectly legal and traceable. That's why he had to ditch it *outside* the hotel."

Joy came to the family room door, wiping her hands on a plaid dishtowel. "You guys ready for dinner?" she asked with a grin.

"Give me three more minutes," Mack said. "I'm explaining something to J.J. Just as soon keep the kids out of it."

She lifted her eyebrows and retreated.

"Where was I? . . . Saturday night. He set up the doors, listening to the headset transmissions to find out where people were. We met him when he was on his way to the north wing to take care of that door, near as I can figure out." Mack shook his head. "Talk about cool.

"He used the missing snake to get Grenzman's headset away. Told him somebody had reported seeing it in the dirty laundry. That's a guess, based on what you heard. Afterwards he rolled the headset up in his costume with the gun, like you said. I located somebody who saw him with the bundle under his arm. It all went into hiding, maybe in the robot. Or—jeez, I never thought of this! Wouldn't it be a gas if he stuck it in a planter with the snake?"

"Might explain why she left," I said.

"Not that smart, I don't think. Snakes, that is. Later, after Yates was interviewed, he retrieved the stuff, put the headset under the mattress in the room Miranda O'Shea had announced would be open and unguarded, and got the gun packed up in the mailer."

"How'd he get that?"

Mack gave me an amused look. "Asked for it. That afternoon."

"Whee," I said.

"I told you he was cool. Where was I, again? Oh." He grimaced. "I'd already given my little speech in the con office, so he'd decided to get rid of April, who might know something from his talk with her."

"Karen's got it all down in her notebook," I said. "Word for word, if I know Karen."

"What?" Mack sat forward, slapping his thighs. I flinched. "You mean to tell me I've been chasing fans all over three states and looking for somebody who might have some idea what he said to April Thorney and *Karen* has it all written down?"

"Most likely. I heard the last couple of sentences, myself."

"J.J."

"They didn't sound like much."

My best friend, my life-long buddy, tilted his head at me and said pleasantly, "One of these days I'm going to wring your neck."

"Hell, Mack, I didn't know he was talking about Maureen!"

"I'll let it by. This time." He studiously unclenched his fists and sat back, making the recliner wheeze. "Anyway, he'd already decided April was too dangerous." Mack turned his head and looked out the window at the darkening yard.

"*He* decided," I said, after a silent moment.

"Yeah," Mack sighed. "Thanks. Well. He couldn't chance another shot, not with the hotel full of cops, so he used the knife, which he'd noticed Saturday morning and grabbed when the lights went out."

Something else the old woman had said came back. Yates didn't have to worry about being found in the service corridor. He was a concom member. If anybody met him he could just say he was looking for the source of the problem with the lights.

"He wanted to mail the gun, but he didn't have stamps. They got a warrant, and it was in that box on the corner, by the way, self-addressed. He didn't want to be noticed asking for them," Mack went on, "and he didn't want to take a chance on just dumping the thing in the mail without stamps on it, so he got April to do it for him. When she came back, he killed her. Then she went into the robot, and he trundled her down to the conference room and hid her under the dais." He glanced at me. "They found blood in it, like we thought."

"Why not just leave her in the robot?" I asked. "Wouldn't that point to Donovan?"

"He didn't know Donovan had been pulling the pranks, and he didn't have any particular quarrel with him. He told Dan Bascombe as late as Sunday morning that he thought all the trouble was due to Grenzman. The business in the kitchen was; the Minneapolis department matched Grenzman's prints with some the rent-a-cops took from the cold room doors that Friday night, Kimski says. Saved Donovan a few more charges. I'm glad. I never could see him doing that."

"Aren't you done yet?" Karen asked, from the kitchen door. "I just finished the gravy."

"One minute," Mack said.

"Hold on," I said. "Karen, remember that conversation you wrote down at the con last month?"

She looked at me blankly.

"After some kind of panel. I found you in that lounge area, and afterward we went to the huckster room."

"Oh. Sure."

"Have you got it written down?"

"*Now*, Joe? Can't it wait?" I shrugged. "Oh, all right.

There'll be no peace till I read it out, I can see that," she said, going to her desk and snatching open a drawer. Mack stared out the back window while she flipped through the pages. "You want it all? It went on for ten minutes, at least."

"No, just tell me if there was anything that might be construed as a threat."

Karen glanced through her notebook, frowning. "Here, he says, 'Sometimes I think I could just kill him. But if he's what she wants . . . ' And here he says, 'He'd better be as clean as he promised Dan he'd be, or there'll be trouble. . . . ' "

"That's enough," I said.

"Dinner now?"

"One minute," Mack said. Karen tossed the notebook onto the desk and went back to the kitchen.

"What about Maureen?" I asked. "How'd she end up at the end of a knife?"

"She figured it out. The mustache. Just like you said, Grenzman used his right hand to draw attention to the right side of the mustache. At least, that's what she thinks, and it makes sense to me. She also knew what we didn't—that Yates was furious with Grenzman over the cocaine, not just because of her but because of the con. So she went and got her knife, concealed it in her jacket pocket, and went after Yates. But he was faster than she was—especially with the hangover she had—and he got the knife away from her. One of the twins walked in to say good-bye two seconds later, or we might not have had that charade in the garage."

"What would we have had?"

"Different corpse at the end, maybe. Who can tell?"

"Pays to stay sober, I guess," I said.

"There's sober, and then there's sober," Mack remarked. He stretched. "Anyway, that's it. Longest weekend of my entire life. And the worst. I don't want to think about it anymore. Ever." He got up, and the recliner sighed in relief. "Karen?" he said at the kitchen door. "Go ahead and call the kids upstairs. Let's have that dinner."

"First you've got to toss the salad," said my wife.

If you have enjoyed this book and would like to receive details of other Walker Mystery-Suspense Novels or join our Crime After Crime Book Club, please write to:

Mystery-Suspense Editor
Walker and Company
720 Fifth Avenue
New York, NY 10019